COWBOY COVER-UP

BARB HAN

TORJAKE PUBLISHING

Editing: Ali Williams

Cover Design: Jacob's Cover Designs

❀ Created with Vellum

To my family for unwavering love and support. I can't imagine doing life with anyone else. I love you guys with all my heart.

"Can you believe that sunset?" The wide-open skies in Texas were always impressive but mother nature was showing off tonight. Brilliant purple and pink brushstrokes painted a cloudless horizon that seemed to go on endlessly. A bright warm orb kissed the hilly green grass that was dotted with wildflowers as sunbeams stretched out like arms.

This day had been just what Alexis Haley needed. Twelve hours in the sun with a friend from work and her sister, and an amazing meal followed by a perfect sunset. *Not bad.*

"I've never seen so many colors in the sky at one time." Angel, her co-worker, was responsible for Alexis's last-minute decision to join the trip.

"If only we could freeze this day and stay here a little bit longer." It would be completely dark soon and despite growing up in Cattle Cove—which was half meadow, half woodland and whole lot ranching territory—Alexis didn't like being outside in the woods after dawn.

"Amazing sunset. Even better wine. Almost makes you forget all your troubles." There was a melancholy note to Angel's voice. She picked up her empty wine glass and smiled. It didn't reach her eyes. "We should probably head in and do dishes."

"Everything okay?"

"It is right now." Angel seemed to catch herself.

"I'll be right in." Alexis wanted another minute on the porch. Being here reminded her of her mother. A twinge of sadness Alexis refused to let take root tugged at her. Dwelling on the past, on her losses, would only send her into a spiral of sadness.

Taking in a deep breath, she shoved the heavy thought aside. She pushed off her chair and made her way inside, thinking her mother wasn't the only person from Cattle Cove she missed.

"I can finish up. Why don't you guys start the movie?" She said to Angel and Darcy.

"Are you sure?" Angel asked, glancing at the ankle Alexis had rolled.

She figured she could stand on one foot just fine. She'd skipped the glass of wine so she could take a painkiller before bed.

"I need a refill," Darcy shouted from the bedroom.

"Go on. I may skip it anyway. Bed sounds really good right now," she said.

Angel nodded and tucked a bottle of wine under her arm. "We'll be in my room if you change your mind."

The cabin had just enough room for the three of them. There was a master bedroom downstairs and a loft that Alexis had gladly agreed to take. She was determined not to let her ankle injury interfere with her first trip in years. There was only one bathroom, but they'd managed okay so far. It was fine for the weekend. This place was more than fine really; it was exactly what she needed.

Angel had made the reservation and paid the most. She took the master bedroom while Darcy negotiated for the pull-out sofa bed. This was supposed to be a sisters' weekend, but Angel had convinced Alexis that getting out of Houston for the weekend was just what she needed. She'd been right. Alexis had been a little skeptical about spending an entire weekend with a co-worker and her sister, but Angel and Darcy were making a real effort to include her.

Honestly, even if they'd left her alone to float around on the lake on her inflatable swan, she would've been fine. There wasn't much that could ruin what had been the perfect day, despite the memories this place dredged up—memories of hanging out here at this lake with her best friend, memories of her mother being alive.

She shoved those thoughts aside. Taking off this weekend had been good for the soul, despite skipping the wine. She wasn't much of a drinker anyway and it gave her an excuse to have iced tea instead.

Alexis finished up the dishes and then swallowed her pill. A quick shower later, and she was ready for bed. The word *tired* didn't begin to describe her current state. She thought about how her new boss had lured her to work at his small marketing agency with the promise of a good work-life balance. That commitment had gone upside down faster than she could say *new job*. Suddenly, a year had passed with almost zero days off.

This weekend was about finally getting a break from campaigns and clients. She'd turned off her cell phone because it felt like an extension of her arm for the past year after the company owner's wife had received a devastating medical diagnosis.

Alexis stretched out long limbs on the soft double bed. Rest and relaxation were the only two items on her agenda.

This area of the cabin must not get used much because it had a slightly musty smell. That didn't bother her, either. Not much did. The painkiller was kicking in. Her ankle had stopped throbbing.

She had just enough sun to wear her out fully. This day had been as close to perfect as she could have hoped. It was strange to be back on McGannon property, though.

Ironically, she'd almost turned down Angel's invitation. Angel had walked over and plopped down on the corner of Alexis's desk like she'd done countless times.

"You're coming with us," she'd said before slapping down a printout of the cabin.

When Alexis had read the familiar address and realized it was owned by her former best friend's family, nostalgia struck. She'd seen it as a sign. Being back at the lake on the land owned by someone from her past reminded her of happier times growing up in Cattle Cove.

Paying attention to the sign had paid off, though. She'd laughed more times in the past twelve hours since they'd checked into the cabin than she had in years. A little piece of her wished Ryan McGannon would have shown up. But that was asking too much and she doubted he thought about her anymore after the way she'd left things. Just being here made her the happiest she'd been in years.

She smiled, letting the thought relax her, despite the fact that, at some point while Alexis was getting ready for bed, Darcy had gone to sleep on the foldout downstairs. She snored so loudly Alexis could swear the walls were shaking. Even that made her laugh.

A NOISE DOWNSTAIRS startled Alexis awake. At first, she thought it was Darcy's snoring, but somewhere in the back of her mind the noise registered as different. She blinked her eyes open. It was dark. *What time was it?*

Her mind was a little fuzzy, but she chalked it up to being half awake. The painkiller she'd taken probably wasn't helping, either.

It took a few seconds to shake the cobwebs. And it took one moment more for her to sit up. She glanced around, trying to get her bearings.

Taking in a deep breath, the musty smell assaulted her. That's right, she was in the loft of the cabin that she'd rented for the weekend with her co-worker.

Alexis listened quietly to see if anyone else was up and moving around downstairs. Whatever sound woke her must not be too important. It was quiet now. She half-figured it was a dream. Maybe she'd snored herself awake like that one embarrassing time in the break room last month when she'd put her head down for a few minutes after eating lunch and then fell asleep hard. A noise woke her then too. Much to her embarrassment, it was the sound of her own snore. Thankfully, she'd been alone. It had been one in a long list of reasons she'd let herself be talked into getting away this weekend.

If she'd stayed home, she would've ended up cleaning her house or grocery shopping, or hanging pictures that were stacked in corners of every room— pictures she'd been meaning to get to since moving closer to work but hadn't had time.

She eased out of the covers and slid her legs over

the side of the bed. Putting any weight on her left ankle caused pain to shoot up her leg. Not wanting to wake Darcy or Angel, she bit back a grunt.

It was still too dark to see much. She blinked her eyes a couple of times trying to adjust to the darkness. She was careful not to make a sound as she tiptoed across the loft. She eased her way down the metal spiral staircase, putting as little pressure on that ankle as she could.

A glance over at Darcy on the foldout said she was dead asleep. At least she'd stopped snoring at some point during the night. Alexis didn't think she'd get a wink of sleep based on how loudly the young woman could snore. But she liked Darcy.

Alexis leaned her hand against the wall and moved toward the bathroom that was in the same hallway as the master. As she rounded the corner into the hallway, she froze.

A large, dark figure was moving inside the bedroom. The person was too big to be Angel.

Someone was inside the cabin. Her heart raced and her pulse skyrocketed.

It was probably just Darcy sneaking in her ex-boyfriend, she reasoned. The two had an on-again, off-again relationship that, according to Darcy, had been going on for the past year. And yet, why would he be in her sister's room?

All Alexis could think was that her cell phone was all the way upstairs if she needed it. She had nothing on her to use as a weapon and the phone was on her nightstand plugged in but turned off.

The floor creaked as she took a step closer to get a better look. She must've gasped without realizing it because before she knew it the dark figure had whirled around and was stalking toward her. He consumed the entire doorway as he passed through, coming at her with all the intensity of a rogue wave during a hurricane.

This was no ex-boyfriend.

"Angel," she called out, taking a couple of steps backward. When there was no answer, she could only pray her co-worker was asleep. Darcy was too quiet.

"You aren't supposed to be here," the dark figure ground out, his voice low and angry.

Alexis screamed as she reached around for the wall, or something to steady her. Her ankle reminded her putting weight on it was a bad idea.

"You won't get away that easy." The unfamiliar low male voice practically growled. The sound sent an icy chill racing down her spine.

"Darcy," she called out desperately, praying for an answer.

None came. That was so not good. Had he given her something? Done something to make her sleep? That would explain why she'd stopped snoring.

There was no way Alexis could make it upstairs to her phone and, besides, she'd be trapped there anyway.

She turned toward the front door and bolted toward it, figuring her best bet was to draw him out of the house. Her ankle screamed in pain and barely supported her weight. Adrenaline spiked and she went numb.

As she reached for the doorknob—her fingers within inches—a thick hand twisted in her hair and jerked her backwards. Her feet left the floor. She screamed until her lungs burned and there was no oxygen left, twisting and fighting the dark figure with arms made from steel.

RYAN MCGANNON TOOK in a deep breath, letting the clean country air fill his lungs. Dawn was his favorite time of day while most of the world was still asleep and the sun would rise over the lake soon in all its glory.

Moments like these were among the many reasons he'd turned down a shot at the minors in favor of working his family's cattle ranch years ago. Some folks, mostly men in town, thought he was crazy for walking away from a chance at working his way toward the majors.

Just because he could throw a baseball didn't mean he wanted to wake up on the road—moving from motel to motel—with very few days off and even less space to breathe. They'd argued that a chance at the majors was like hitting the Lotto. Ryan took another look around. In his mind, he'd already won. And money was just that...money. It didn't make a person happy. Working with his hands and building on his family's legacy did. Besides, a roof over his head at night and a decent meal on the table was all Ryan needed.

Out here, he didn't have to be around people for days. He could stretch out his legs and ride his horse whenever he pleased.

On the road, he would have been grabbing every minute of shuteye that he could. There'd be no time to appreciate sunrises like the one he was about to enjoy.

Now, that would've been a shame. Besides, a career in sports never lasted long. He paused long enough to admire the view.

Out here, Ryan could think.

He didn't condemn anyone who wanted that dream. Hard work was always respectable, and he knew better than most how hard players worked in the minors trying to get a shot at something bigger. A couple of his friends had gone down that path and a whole lot more wished they could've. Many people had the dream of playing professional sports at one time in their lives. He just wasn't one of them. Ranching was in his heart and in his blood.

After the sun made an appearance, he'd check on the cabin his brother had talked the family into using as a weekend rental. A young couple had rented the place for years, but now that they were expecting their first child, they'd opted to move closer to town for convenience.

Rogue shifted at Ryan's feet. The German shepherd been brought to the property in bad shape as a pup four years ago. But now, stronger than ever, he stood by Ryan's side as he stared out onto the vastness that was McGannon Herd Cattle Ranch.

Ryan volunteered to take this side of the property this morning, not at all thrilled his family had decided to rent out the cabin to weekenders. He didn't want or need the headache that would come with young people on his family's land. Granted, this wasn't an ideal location for hunting, and this place was too close to the big house anyway to be useful for the family. Even so, Ryan wasn't convinced rental was the way to go. A.J., however, had enough confidence in the plan for both of them. He'd decided the cabin was better off used. He'd made a good argument. Walk by any unused playground and it was easy to see all kinds of bad elements settled in. It probably wasn't the smartest move to leave the cabin vacant. It would invite teens or anyone else passing through to do break in or vandalize the place. He and his brothers would have to look after the cabin anyway and A.J. had suggested they find a way to make money when no one was using it for fishing. The problem with using it as a rental was that he didn't want to deal with parties and obnoxious drunks. He'd been voted down and his older brother

A.J. had put the cabin out on some rental site. Ryan hadn't found a good enough counterargument to the idea, so he'd reluctantly gone along with it. Wouldn't stop him from checking on the cabin, though, and that's exactly what he was doing.

The place seemed quiet enough.

Rogue's ears shot up. He listened for something. Ryan had no idea what. His dog was becoming restless and that wasn't like him. Eyes and ears on alert, something had his attention. Did he smell food? Ryan was convinced his dog could sniff out bacon from two counties over.

Rogue had been named for his tendency to take off without warning. Ryan kept an eye on his rescue dog.

"We'll get home in time for breakfast," Ryan reassured. He'd never once missed feeding his dog and yet Rogue still got nervous when mealtime was close and they were out on the property.

At least, Ryan thought hunger was the problem. Rogue had been rescued from a breeding operation that kept him locked in a cage his first year and Ryan had been asked to keep him for a few days until the rescue organization found a proper home. The two had been inseparable ever since.

The wind kicked up a notch and Rogue's ears perked up. His body stiffened as he pointed his snout in the direction of the cabin. And then he bolted.

2

"Dammit, Rogue." Ryan had only meant to get a visual on the cabin to make sure no one had burned the place down. His dog was about to bust him for being there. He could only hope the occupants would be passed out and that he could retrieve his dog without waking anyone. He'd get in and out of the area, and no one would be the wiser. At least that had been the plan until now. If Rogue got close to whatever he was chasing, his barking would wake the renters.

A.J. would read Ryan the riot act. Since he didn't want an earful from his brother, Ryan started toward the dog, who was at a dead run. He whistled but Rogue wasn't having it.

Ryan cursed again under his breath, figuring he needed to think up a good excuse to be out keeping tabs on the cabin. And then he heard a blood-curdling scream. Rogue's barks came out rapid-fire now.

Without hesitation, Ryan bolted toward the noise full force. He tried to convince himself the renter had come across a spider, something he could easily help with. His excuse for being in the area would be a morning walk. He could always float the *checking fences* excuse. It wasn't a lie. He'd planned to check fences while he was here.

Another scream sent an icy chill down his back. Instinct told him this was no spider.

There was just enough light for him to see Rogue make it to the cabin and disappear around the corner. Ryan had another twenty-five yards to go. He pushed his legs until his thighs burned. And then he heard a sound come from the opposite side of the cabin, a dirt bike engine being gunned.

He released a string of curses as he sprinted harder, wishing he had half of Rogue's speed.

As he rounded the corner, he saw a woman scrambling to get to her feet on the front porch. Her head was turned toward the sound of the motorcycle and the direction Rogue had gone.

She favored her right leg as she gripped the exterior wall of the log cabin. She looked unsteady on her feet and her chest was heaving like she'd been in a fight. His first thought was a fight with her boyfriend but the screams he heard a few seconds ago didn't sound like the result of a heated argument with someone she knew. They sounded like she was fighting for her life.

"Ma'am," Ryan shouted to announce his presence, not wanting to scare her any more than she already was.

When she turned to face him, shock registered.

"Ryan?" The moment of nostalgia was quickly quashed by her next words. "Help us. We need an ambulance. My friends are inside…"

She didn't seem as shocked to see him as he expected, but then she had the advantage of knowing she was on McGannon property. He wasn't told Alexis Haley was their renter. Then again, he hadn't asked.

"What's happened?" Ryan had his cell phone out in a heartbeat. One look at her and his chest squeezed. It had been a long time and hers was a face he never expected to see again.

Her face was sheet white and her body was trembling. He stared into panicked eyes.

"I honestly don't know. I was asleep one minute and the next this guy was downstairs in Angel's bedroom. He saw me and came after me. It all happened so fast after that. I tried to get him away from the cabin. He caught me." She glanced at the front door. "If they were all right wouldn't they be awake by now?" Her eyes pleaded. "Something bad has happened in there, Ryan. They aren't moving."

"Drinking?" He had to ask.

"A glass of wine and that was hours ago." She

reached for the screen door and almost lost her balance.

He made a move to help but she sidestepped his hand, moving out of reach.

"I'm okay. But they need help. No one's come out of there and they didn't wake up when I screamed. I'm afraid something's very wrong with them, Ryan."

Didn't that send another cold shiver racing down his back.

"Who else is inside?" he asked.

"Just Darcy on the couch and Angel in the master as far as I know," she said. He wanted to get more information, but she looked like she was about to burst into tears and was barely holding it together.

He hit the last number of 9-1-1.

"Can you tell the dispatcher what happened for me? Ask for an ambulance and the sheriff, okay?" He handed the phone over to her and whistled for his dog. Ryan scanned the tree line, looking for signs of movement. There was none.

He whistled again, hoping a second time would do the trick. A few tense seconds later, Rogue came bursting out of the scrub brush.

Ryan issued a sharp sigh and opened the screen door. Nothing could prepare him for the stillness inside the cabin or the feeling of death that struck him as he walked inside. There wasn't so much as a faucet dripping and the quiet was eerie enough to cause the hairs on the back of his neck to stand on end.

Ryan took a step forward and stopped, realizing this was a crime scene and he wanted to be careful not to destroy evidence. Alexis practically walked into him. He didn't mind that he'd picked up a shadow. Or that she stayed glued to him as he entered the cabin.

To his right, on the fold-out sofa, he saw a lifeless body. A pillow looked as though it had been pressed into her face. Her arms and legs had fallen in odd angles.

"One of my friends is dead and I don't know about the other," Alexis said into the phone right behind him.

Ryan immediately scanned the area, looking for the possibility of a second intruder.

"Just one?" he asked Alexis out of the side of his mouth.

"That's all I know about," she said. He hated that her voice was shaking. He could feel her body trembling behind him.

Rogue had wedged himself in between the two of them. He'd witnessed animals stepping up to act as comfort for humans countless times and it still left him in awe.

"Yes, ma'am." Alexis continued her conversation with the dispatcher. "My friend is Darcy Ward. She's on the couch bed in the living room. I was sleeping in the loft of a cabin we rented on the McGannon ranch. Whoever was here hadn't gone upstairs yet. He was in the master bedroom with my friend Angel when I interrupted him."

Ryan started taking mental inventory. The front door was open. There were no signs of forced entry. He'd touched the handle of the screen door and that was unfortunate. He might've covered any fingerprint evidence there.

He moved stealthily into the bedroom where another body lay still. A pillow covered her face and the sheets were in a tangle like she'd fought hard and lost. The scene was eerily similar to the living room.

Nothing else looked out of place as he skimmed the bedroom. He took a step inside and noticed a cell phone and charger had been knocked off the night-stand. He moved to the first person, Angel, and checked for a pulse. There was none, so he needed to get Alexis out of there.

In the living room, he got more of the same.

A double murder that could have ended up a triple homicide. Ryan's mind raced with possibilities.

"Tell me everything you remember," he said.

She ran it down for him. There'd been an intruder. She'd heard a noise. She was still groggy from taking a painkiller the night before, for an injured left ankle. That explained the limp. She came downstairs to use the bathroom. Thought her friend's sister was asleep on the couch. Noticed that the sister had stopped snoring. Rounded the corner to the only bathroom in the small cabin. Realized there was an intruder. It was still dark. She was impaired from the medicine.

The description of the intruder was that he was big. He seemed bulky. He filled the doorframe as he came toward her from the bedroom. She'd heard his voice. She'd turned to run, trying to draw him out of the cabin and away from her friend and the sister.

He followed. Jerked her backwards by her hair. By then, she'd started screaming. She forced herself out onto the porch by sheer force of will, despite the strong hands trying to jolt her backward.

Somehow, she managed to kick him where no man wanted a foot. In a second, he was on the porch and at the same time a dog started barking. The intruder must've realized the dog had an owner and the guy feared he was about to get busted, or he was just straight up afraid of Rogue. The animal looked fierce and he could be deadly when he wanted to be. He went after the guy, but he'd already made it to the scrub bush where he'd tucked something that sounded more like a dirt bike than a motorcycle.

A dirt bike made more sense in the woods anyway.

One glance at Alexis and Ryan's heart clenched. She had a vulnerability to her in that moment that brought all his protective instincts to life. It brought him back to the devastation she'd felt as a teenager and he'd been unable to stop. All made worse by the fact that Alexis Haley was one of the last people he'd clas-

between them. A decade may have passed since they'd been friends and they might have left on bad terms, but that didn't matter now. What she wanted didn't need to be spelled out. He didn't have to know her like the back of his hand to know what she wanted. Comfort.

He pulled her toward him and was assaulted by her scent, all flowers and citrus. He wrapped his arms around her, and she buried her face in his chest.

"You're safe now. It's over." They both knew the shock and pain of this ordeal would last a lifetime, but this was the time for reassurance.

She didn't cry. He wouldn't expect her to. All she did was stand there while her body trembled. Despite the already warm temperatures, she shook like she was standing outside without a coat in twenty-degree weather.

This had to be from shock.

He'd heard her tell the dispatcher that she had no idea who the intruder was and that she didn't get a very good look at him, either. More of that frustration seethed as Ryan recounted her story in his mind.

She was lucky to be alive. But then *lucky* was a relative term. She sure as hell wasn't lucky to have been at the cabin overnight.

Considering she didn't know the intruder, he assumed she wasn't the target. But then, if this was random, the fact that she'd slept in the loft most likely saved her life.

Most of the time, an ex was to blame in violent crimes against women. It was anyone's guess in this case until the sheriff and her deputies investigated.

A trail of dust and the growing roar of sirens signaled help was almost there.

Deputy Mark Tucker 'Tuck' roared up to the scene first in his department-issued SUV. He was in his late thirties and insisted everyone call him by the nickname he'd grown up with. He was the oldest of three kids and the only boy in the Tucker family. His youngest sister, Mallie, had been a grade above Ryan and Alexis.

Alexis took a step back, so Ryan hopped off the porch and met Tuck halfway. The two shook hands.

"The suspect took off in that direction." Ryan pointed toward the wooded area. "There are two bodies inside the cabin, both females."

Tuck winced.

"Ambulance is right behind me." True to Tuck's word, another squall of dust clouds came at them. The red and white ambulance emerged, pulling up right beside Tuck's SUV.

A pair of EMTs came bolting out and made a beeline toward Tuck, who quickly excused himself and lead the pair of emergency workers inside the cabin.

Alexis was shaking her head, and Ryan realized immediately that she was saying she couldn't go back inside. Ryan had no plans to be the one to force her to face that place again.

"I need my phone," she said as Rogue sat next to her leg. The five-year-old German shepherd had missed his calling as a sidekick. He would have made an excellent therapy dog. With his body leaning against her leg, she seemed comforted at a level well below panic.

And based on what she'd witnessed inside his family's cabin, she was going to need twenty-four-seven support. Somehow, he doubted she'd see it that way, so it was going to be up to him to convince her.

3

"We can ask Tuck to bring your phone out," Ryan's voice was calm, and it was helping to calm Alexis. "He might want to keep it for evidence, though."

"Good point." Alexis wasn't thinking clearly. She needed to get her bearings and come up with a plan. The reality of the situation struck hard. Looking at the SUV and the ambulance made everything so much more real and yet a part of her held onto the hope none of this was really happening. "He killed them, Ryan." She said the words out loud more for her benefit than his.

"I know." Those two words were spoken with such gentleness her heart squeezed.

Shock was wearing thin and the reality of what had just happened was starting to sink in. Alexis figured there was no way she could process everything and especially not Angel and her sister being murdered. That was too much for any one person to absorb. She needed time.

"Their parents are still married and alive in Houston." She started to sink down but was held up by a strong hand. She ignored the sensual shiver racing across her skin with contact. "This is it. Angel and Darcy were the only two siblings in their family."

She said the words barely in a whisper. The cabin was a crime scene now. Everything would need to be examined. Evidence would need to be collected and analyzed. Their parents would have to be notified. She couldn't imagine the horror for a parent to lose not only one but both children in one moment.

The bastard responsible needed to be caught and locked up for the rest of his life. Justice needed to be served.

"What did he say to you?" Ryan asked, his voice bringing her out of her heavy thoughts. "You said you heard the intruder's voice."

"That I shouldn't be here." A shiver rocked through her at remembering his words and the sound of his voice.

"You said you didn't recognize him." He seemed to be studying her.

It had been so long since she'd even thought about him, having done her best to forget all about Ryan McGannon after their argument. Now, wasn't the time to bring up the past, *their* past. Besides, what had gone down between them had happened such a long time ago. She doubted he even cared or remembered at this point.

And yet, seeing him again stirred up emotions that she'd tucked away along with those memories of him —memories that had been so damn good. There'd been so many times when she'd wondered exactly what this moment would be like. Would they feel like strangers? Would all that hurt come roaring back? Or would it seem like nothing had changed and they could pick up where they left off before the fight?

"No. I mean, he spoke so low and his words came out more like an animal growling at me so I can't be certain of anything." It also meant she couldn't pick the guy out of a lineup or identify his real tone if she walked past him on the street. The thought caused an icy chill to race down her spine. She tried to take a step, needing to get out some of her nervous tension, and her ankle gave. She managed a quick hop to keep herself from falling but that ankle was angry.

"Do you want to sit down inside Tuck's SUV?" Ryan put his arm around her to steady her.

She nodded and he helped her over to the vehicle. She climbed into the passenger side. As it was, she felt like her left ankle might give out. It was probably a good idea to sit even though she wanted to move around, to pace.

And she wanted the hell out of the clothes she was

wearing. Everything felt awful against her skin and she wanted nothing more than to get her pajamas off and burn every stitch of clothing on her body.

A dark thought struck. Those were probably evidence now too.

It was probably the shock of events that had her wanting to reach out to something familiar, to some*one* familiar. Ryan certainly fit that bill. She hadn't seen or heard from him in what felt like forever.

Over the years, he'd grown from a wiry and tall teen into a muscled, athletic man. He'd filled out that six-foot-three-inch frame with solid rock. His brown hair had darkened almost to black and he had the most intense dark roast coffee colored eyes.

The terms *built, tall* and *muscled* definitely applied. It was probably just being back in Cattle Cove again that had her feeling all nostalgic, but seeing Ryan again felt better than she should let it. Because once this was over with, he'd be gone again too.

"It's good to see you again, Alexis. I'm sorry about the circumstances. Everything about this is awful," he said with enough sincerity to make her heart fill.

"Same to you, Ryan. When I heard we were going to be staying on your family's property, it made me feel like I was coming home in a weird way." She stopped there because she didn't see the need to go into memories of them camping out at this very lake. "I have to say that I was surprised your family was renting out this place."

"Not my idea." His answer came quick and his words sounded curt. His irritation came through loud and clear. End of subject.

"Well, maybe not everyone has changed since I left town."

His smile didn't reach his eyes, but she appreciated the attempt. "Are you saying that I can be stubborn?"

"All I know is mules get a bad rep when it comes to being compared to you." It felt surprisingly good to talk about something normal for a minute to distract her mind from what was going on inside the cabin.

The feeling lasted all of about thirty seconds before Tuck came out and started stretching out crime scene tape across the door. The situation was becoming so much more real and her mind was beginning to accept the fact that this wasn't a nightmare.

Tuck finished up and walked over to them.

"We're going to be here for some time," Tuck began. "I'd like to get a statement from you while the details are fresh on your mind, if you're up to it."

Alexis nodded. She wanted to do anything and everything possible to help find the bastard responsible as quickly as possible. The thought he could strike again weighed heavily on her chest.

"Excuse me while I make a call to the big house and let my family know what's going on," Ryan said before fishing his cell from his pocket and holding it up.

Tuck nodded and Ryan took a couple of steps away

from them. His absence caused a stab of panic in her chest.

Thankfully, he stopped and turned. Seeing his profile calmed her enough that she was able to give her statement. Having someone familiar around kept her nerves from taking over and running away with her emotions.

Another deputy drove up and Tuck waved him into the crime scene without leaving the vehicle.

"Tell me in your own words everything you remember." Tuck moved into the driver's seat and positioned his laptop so he could type straight into the system while she spoke.

She ran through the details. It didn't take more than fifteen minutes to tell him everything she knew. She also realized that she didn't have very much information to give. "I'm sorry there isn't more. I wish I could have…"

Her voice broke on the last word. She tucked her chin to her chest to hide the tears that were welling in her eyes.

"It's not your fault." Tuck spoke with such calm finality that she almost believed him. And yet it still felt like somehow it was. "What were the three of you doing here in Cattle Cove?"

"Taking a weekend off and bonding. I've been working at my job for a little more than a year. Angel and I are co-workers. Darcy's her younger sister." She had to pause as emotion tried to get the best of her. "Anyway, our owner's wife was diagnosed with lymphoma, so it's been a pretty rough go the last year. My work schedule hasn't left a whole lot of time to have a personal life. While we're at work, we're pretty much heads down and none of us have taken more than half a day off since the diagnosis came. My co-worker thought it would be a good idea to rent the cabin and get out of town for a weekend now that the owner's sister-in-law came to relieve him. She'd been planning this trip with her sister and asked me to come along so we could get to know each other and, I suspect, split the bill."

"That's understandable," Tuck said with a sympathetic smile.

She looked down and her heart swelled at the fact Ryan's dog hadn't left her side.

"Did you say you live in Houston now?" Tuck asked.

"Yes, sir. I've been living there ever since I left Cattle Cove. I moved there to live with my cousin after my mom died." She couldn't help but think death seemed to follow her.

"I'm sorry about your mom." Tuck spoke with more of that compassion. Despite his sincerity, it didn't have the same effect as Ryan's.

"Thank you," she said, and meant it. She'd take all the generosity she could get.

"How well did you know your co-worker or her sister before this weekend?" Tuck asked.

"As well as anyone can know someone they work with every day. We ordered lunch in most of the time and ate at our desks more often than not, so we could go home on time and get some sleep. I knew her well enough to realize her favorite color was green. She wore it a lot and it went really well with her red hair, which was part natural and a lot from a bottle." She needed to stop for another second before continuing. Her mouth had dried up and talking was hard.

"Would you like a bottle of water, Ms. Haley?" Tuck asked.

"Please, call me Alexis. I know we didn't *know* each other but we were around each other most of my youth. It's weird to have someone so familiar speak to me so properly," she admitted. It was probably her nerves talking, wanting more of the familiar because she felt so alien right then.

Everything was surreal.

"Okay, Alexis. Just don't tell my boss. She likes to follow protocol despite growing up here along with the rest of us." He winked and it was meant to lighten the mood, so she smiled.

"To answer your questions, I'd rather have coffee than water but that's probably not a possibility." A dull throb was forming in the spot right in between her eyes. Her body craved caffeine, but she didn't want anything from that house but her purse and her phone.

"Have you or any of your co-workers been in a fight with anyone that you know of? Ex-boyfriend? Friend?" Tuck continued the questioning thread.

"Darcy had a boyfriend. She had a bad breakup and that's part of the reason her sister thought it would be a good idea to get away. Apparently, the relationship was on and off, and her sister didn't think it was healthy."

The way Tuck rocked his head and how quickly his fingers danced across the keyboard told her she'd hit a hot button.

"Did Darcy mention her ex-boyfriend's name?" Tuck looked up and made eye contact.

"All I know is that his first name is Stevie. She referred to him that way a lot. I don't have a last name." It was also embarrassing to admit that when it came to Darcy and Angel, she didn't know a whole lot of personal details about them, either. That was part of what this weekend was supposed to be about. Bonding.

Thinking about this news being delivered to their parents caused the air to thin and her chest to squeeze. Knowing the amount of pain that the people who cared about them were about to endure caused her stomach to cramp. She knew loss. Her mother had been her lifeline through difficult teenage years despite working nights as a nurse and barely being around. And yet, her mother had always managed to be there for the important moments.

There was only one thing she could think of that could be worse than breaking the Pruitt's hearts, and that was having no one at all who would really care if she lived or died.

Granted, her cousin and his wife wouldn't exactly jump for joy if anything happened to Alexis. But since she'd moved out years ago, they barely kept in touch. He was busy with his young family and she had her work.

Having no one who would truly miss her hit hard.

"What about Angel? Did she get along with everyone at work?" Tuck continued.

"As far as I know. I mean there was always a little bit of bickering when people work long hours and miss their family. Arguments about who should get Saturday night off or come in early on Sunday. Angel was pretty quiet about her personal life actually, but I don't think she was seeing anyone."

Ryan ended the call he'd been on and moved to her side. Warmth blanketed her with him so close. It was almost enough to stop her from body from trembling.

"And you? Are you seeing—"

"Nope. No boyfriend for me." She cut him off, unsure of why admitting that in front of Ryan made her cheeks burn. Without thinking much about her next actions, she glanced at Ryan's finger on his left hand and relief—relief that was confusing—washed over her when she saw no band there. It was silly to be possessive about Ryan because nothing had ever happened between them besides friendship and they hadn't spoken in years.

She chalked her embarrassment up to revealing how little of a life she had and moved on. Or, at least she tried to.

4

Ryan stood by and watched as Alexis made a list of everyone she knew, as well as all known associates of Angel and her sister, Darcy. Tension lines formed, leaving deep grooves in her forehead. Her face muscles were tight, and she kept touching that spot above her eyes that generally meant she was getting one of her headaches, which wasn't good.

The migraines had started not long after her mother had been killed in a car crash. They'd get so bad she'd have to close herself off in a dark room for the rest of the day. Ryan's father had quietly arranged for Alexis to stay in town at the bed and breakfast owned by Camilla Brown's family. That way, she could finish her final few weeks of senior high school in Cattle Cove.

There'd been no point digging into old wounds—

wounds that had festered until they never talked anymore despite how close they'd been. Friendships didn't always last forever and she'd been clear when she'd stomped off and never looked back, that she'd been done with him.

In hindsight, she'd systematically pushed everyone away after losing her mother. Ryan's father had told him to give her space when he'd asked his old man for advice. Maybe it wasn't his smartest move. Maybe she'd needed to know how important she was and that she had people who cared about her.

His family wasn't the kiss and cry together type. He'd always known he could count on his brothers for anything he needed. It went without saying. But they never sat around the dinner table or in the family room and talked anything out.

When anger got the best of Ryan, he'd head straight to the barn and sign up for physical labor with Hawk or hit the gym at school early for an intense workout. Words had never been his specialty.

They weren't then and he couldn't say he'd gotten any better now. By the time he'd figured out a way to make amends with Alexis at graduation, she'd skipped the ceremony. Next thing he knew, she'd moved to Houston to live with her cousin without saying a word.

Trying to reach her had done no good. She'd changed her cell number and a big part of him wondered if she'd done it to close the door to her past completely. Like talking to him would only make the pain of losing her mom and her life in Cattle Cove that much harder. At least, that's how his immature eighteen-year-old brain had interpreted it.

Granted, they'd been in a fight, but he thought they'd talk it out. Apparently, she had other ideas.

A part of him, and maybe it was just wishful thinking, made him think she'd pushed the whole world away all those years ago and not just him. It was probably just wounded pride talking to soothe his bruised ego at being rejected by someone he'd considered a friend.

He'd been young and naïve and figured she'd call when she was ready to talk. Days had turned into weeks. Weeks into months. Months into years.

She'd been the one in control and she'd never made the call to patch up their friendship. Of course, he would handle the entire situation differently now that he was an adult. But his stubborn high school heart had been deeply offended when she'd pushed him away. Thinking he'd been right; he'd dug his heels in and lost a friend.

The fight they had over who was going to pick up the other for school hadn't seemed like something that would drive a wedge between them that would last years.

There'd been countless times he'd wanted to find a way to clear the air, when he'd given her space instead. After a year passed with no word from her, he figured she'd moved on and decided it would be for the best if he followed suit. It took some time, but eventually he had moved on, too.

Seeing her now brought a flood of emotions threatening to drag him under—emotions he chalked up to collateral damage from their past. The way she'd left things had confused him. Hell, they'd been teenagers. What had they known?

Years had disappeared and the distance between them had spread.

Looking at her now, a small piece of him couldn't help but wish life had turned out differently and especially for her. Losing her one and only parent so early in life must've played a number on her. Ryan couldn't completely relate until recently, when his own father had been found unconscious in the barn by his uncle. His Uncle Donny had turned up at the ranch a few years ago after blowing his considerable inheritance and had been trouble ever since.

Ryan's father wasn't the type to turn his back on family, so he'd given Donny a job. The move had caused a ripple in the family that was growing into a chasm. Despite loving their five cousins, Ryan and his brothers didn't trust their uncle as far as they could throw him.

Another dust cloud formed as Hawk Jenkins drove up to the cabin in his work pickup.

Hawk was a godsend. He'd been ranch foreman for longer than Ryan had been out of diapers and was practically family. Ryan walked over to Hawk as he exited the truck and offered a handshake. Hawk pulled Ryan into a bear hug. He was just that kind of guy when it came to Ryan and his brothers. Not so much with people he would view as outsiders.

Hawk was closer to Ryan's father's age. He'd picked up the name Hawk based the fact nothing got past him. The man's size was deceiving. He had the strength of an ox. Ryan wouldn't want to be on the wrong end of a fight with Hawk despite the age and size difference between them. Hawk could hold his own. He had street smarts from his time as a rough young kid growing up in San Antonio in government housing. He'd said many times that finding his calling as a ranch hand and then ranch foreman had saved his life. His love of animals had given him purpose when he'd given up on people.

And no amount of money could buy the kind of loyalty he gave to the McGannon family. They'd embraced him as one of their own and he'd often joked that he had six sons despite never being married or having children.

The feeling was mutual.

"I brought what you requested," Hawk said.

Hawk reached into the backseat of his truck and produced a carafe and a pair of cups. "Wasn't sure how anyone took it, so I brought it black. There's a milk carton if anyone needs it."

"You're a lifesaver, Hawk." Ryan took the offerings and walked over to where Alexis had pen to paper.

"When I was on the phone, I heard you mention that you'd like a cup of coffee." He held up the carafe.

Alexis glanced up. Her eyes widened and her tongue darted across her bottom lip, leaving a silky trail. "Are you kidding? Is that for real?"

"How do you take it?"

"At this point, I'm not one to be picky. I'd take cream if you had it," she said.

"I can make that happen for you." His chest swelled with pride at being able to give her a little sense of normalcy after the ordeal she'd been through.

Ryan moved back to Hawk's truck and poured two cups. He left enough room for cream in Alexis's cup. He remembered that she'd always taken it that way but wasn't sure how much had changed in the years since they'd known each other.

In some ways, seeing her again was like looking at a stranger. But then a moment like this helped him see the person he'd known was still in there. Parts of her might be buried deep but still remained.

It was good that some things about her hadn't changed.

When he brought over the fresh brew, she exhaled. She took the cup and blew on top of the liquid. Steam rolled off.

She took a sip, looking like she enjoyed the burn on her throat. And then her gaze locked onto his.

"I can't thank you enough, Ryan. This definitely qualifies as above and beyond the call of duty." She glanced around before taking another sip. "This is probably the best cup of coffee I've ever had in my life."

He figured it was the circumstances talking, more than the quality of the brew, but he would take it either way. A part of him that had been buried too long liked making Alexis happy. He might not know what she'd been up to for the past few years, but losing her mother at such a critical age would do a number on anyone. He could see that so clearly now.

Back when he was younger and she started pushing him away, he'd taken it personally. If only he could go back, he would do things so differently.

Too late now. He couldn't undo the arguments or his lack of understanding. His own mother had died when he was too young to know what he'd missed out on. And he'd had his father, who'd been his rock.

Between his brothers and cousins, Ryan had always had someone around who cared about him. Looking at Alexis now, it struck him just how alone she must've been. Throw in all those confusing teenage hormones, which made life hard on someone with all the advantages, and it was shocking that she'd turned out so well.

But then, this was Alexis. She'd always been strong.

Looking back, she'd put her head down and a wall up. From the looks of it, not much had changed. She was still trying to shoulder everything on her own rather than reach out for help.

"I've literally written down every person I know who has come into contact with Angel." She tapped her pen on the notepad. "I didn't know Darcy well enough to make a list for her."

"I'm sure that her parents will be able to fill in the gaps."

"I just keep thinking about them, Ryan. They're getting older. I met them at the company Christmas party. They seemed like sweet people." She paused and ducked her chin to her chest.

He gave her a minute.

She cleared her throat, took a sip of coffee and continued, "No parent should have to learn their child was murdered."

"It's against the natural order of things for a child to die before his or her parents. Even if that child is considered an adult," he agreed.

Ryan couldn't imagine the level of hell that would come with losing a child. All he knew for certain was that it seemed like a cruel twist of fate.

"Are you happy with your life in Houston?" Ryan couldn't help but ask.

"Yeah, I guess so." She shrugged; her gaze still focused on the sheet of paper. She'd drawn two lines, separating out the page into three equal parts. At the top of each part, she'd written a name; hers, Angel and Darcy.

Ryan couldn't help but notice how few names she'd written under her own.

"Other than your work situation. I mean...personally." He treated lightly as the tapping of the pen hit double time.

"Maybe it's best if we don't talk about that right now, Ryan." Her words were so final that he felt another layer of wall come up in between them.

PULLING from whatever strength she had left, Alexis kept her gaze on the paper. There was something eye opening about looking at her list of friends and realizing they were all co-workers. Those were generally classified as circumstantial friends. The circumstances changed and so did the friendships. Those quickly morphed into social media acquaintances, people who dropped an occasional comment or like on a post. Then again, Alexis had never been big on posting her life events.

Social media only reminded her how small her life was. The few birthday celebration invites she'd received had dwindled this past year to nil. She understood. Friendships took an investment of time. Relationships were complicated and couldn't just be put on autopilot. They required nurturing she didn't have the energy for after a long day at work. Besides, she'd probably lost her touch with people anyway. The last guy she'd been on a date with hadn't cared that she was coming off a string of twelve hours days when he'd told her that she was boring. It wasn't all his fault. She had dozed off when he stepped away from the table for a few minutes to return a phone call.

Maybe she should start by trying to keep a plant alive.

A third SUV pulled up on the driver's side and it was marked with the word, SHERIFF. Ryan aimed his camera at her pad of paper and took a snap after making eye contact and her giving him the nod.

Alexis recognized the woman who emerged from the vehicle as she walked over. Laney Justice had been a few grades ahead of Alexis in school. The sheriff looked to be around five-feet-two-inches. Despite her height, she walked with authority and it was easy to see she was confident that she could handle herself in any situation.

"My name is Laney." The sheriff offered a hand-shake as Ryan stepped aside presumably to let the two of them talk.

Alexis liked that he stayed close by. She could use a friend and being with one who had a shared history was nicer than she expected it to be. Shutting off anything and everything that had reminded her of home, and her mother, had been her way of surviving the tragedy and the forced changes in her life at the time.

"I'm Alexis Haley." She took the outstretched hand.

The sheriff turned her attention to Ryan next, acknowledging his presence by greeting him and offering a handshake. "This is McGannon property, right?"

"Yes. I'm a representative for the family," he said. Hearing that he might be here as part of his duty and not because of their past friendship felt like a knife stab to the chest. Breathing hurt.

Of course, that would be the reason he'd stuck around and not out of some sense of their shared past. It made perfect sense when she really thought about it. This was McGannon land. Someone from the family needed to be here to speak to authorities. A double murder had occurred and no McGannon would take that lightly.

Her chest shouldn't deflate at the realization Ryan was just doing his job and yet that's exactly what happened. The reminder not to get too comfortable around him was needed because she felt a tug toward opening up to him and letting him in a little bit.

The feeling was dangerous. He'd hurt her once and he'd do it again. She doubted he even knew how devastated she'd been all those years ago after their fight. Separating out her feelings about her mother's death from the moment she realized she'd be leaving Cattle Cove and her best friend had proved difficult.

"Can I ask what made you and your friends decide to come to the ranch?" Justice asked.

Alexis wasn't sure she wanted to answer that question.

5

"Good question. I came because Angel talked me into it. She came to me last minute and convinced me it would be a good idea to get away for a weekend. Said it wouldn't cost much if we split it three ways." Alexis didn't want to explain her real reasoning of needing to be close to the McGannon ranch again.

The sheriff nodded. She seemed well-meaning.

Hearing herself talk about jumping at the chance to come back to Cattle Cove and the chance to run into Ryan again seemed misinformed to her now, especially since he'd shown up out of duty.

The horrific event that had occurred left her unsure of how to feel, except from a nagging feeling that the only people whom she'd let in even just a little bit were now dead. A little voice in the back of her mind tried to remind her that it wasn't her fault. But there was no room for logic in times of overwrought emotion.

She wanted to go home except that she didn't even know where that was anymore. Houston should come to mind, but her small house still wasn't unpacked, and if she was being completely honest it never had felt like *home.*

It wasn't Houston's fault. It was a great city. Alexis just hadn't had that *home* feeling since losing her mother. Since Cattle Cove. And, just recently, since seeing Ryan again.

Alexis's chest constricted and she froze up. It took a little while, despite taking a pain killer that normally knocked her on her bottom, but she refocused her thoughts using the deep breathing technique she'd learned from her counselor. Seeing a therapist after losing her mother had been her cousin's idea. All the loss, all the changes had caused panic attacks that had derailed her. Understanding what was happening to her mind and body while developing tools to handle the tsunami was the reason she'd come this far.

Eric had taken Alexis in and given her a bedroom after she'd graduated high school with nowhere to go. He was ten years older than her and had a new marriage and a baby on the way.

Keeping her head down was the best way not to interfere with his life. Working as a waitress while taking classes had made a two-year degree take four. It had paid off, though. She'd gotten a job that paid more than minimum wage or relied on tips, which could be sketchy.

A couple of months into her new job, she'd saved enough for a down payment on a used car and a security deposit on a new apartment. Furniture had come piece by piece. She'd slept on a mattress on the floor her first year and loved every bit of independence that came with it.

Eric had gotten four years of free babysitting out of the deal, which he'd apparently taken for granted while she lived with him and his wife. He seemed to realize how lucky he was to have a built-in babysitter when he tried to guilt her to move back following the birth of his second child. If he hadn't been so demanding while she'd been in school, she might've considered it. Plus, the fact him and his wife always made her feel like a fifth wheel. She'd paid her dues, and then some, in changing diapers and washing dishes while under his roof. She'd been put into the middle of the night feeding rotation and covered weekly date nights.

When she'd moved out, she was done. She'd never asked for a handout and didn't mind working her behind off in exchange for a roof over her head. She'd contributed money for food and made enough to pay for her classes and a bus pass.

Working non-stop since then had been a breeze. This day had been a long time coming. Not even the sweltering mid-September temperatures or the fact that she'd twisted her already injured ankle hard could keep the smile off her face tonight as she drifted off.

Friends had been few and far between since she'd had almost no time or extra money in years. That was all changing now. The situation with her boss was temporary. And she had enough money saved to make her next move, which was a down payment on a little bungalow in the suburbs north of the city.

Angel and Darcy coming into her life had been icing on the cake. The friendship might be new but she's liked them both. Angel was a peanut counter, a.k.a. financial person at the marketing company where they worked.

"Did she say why she chose this cabin to rent in the first place?" The sheriff asked.

"It wasn't a long drive from Houston where we live. Angel said someone had recommended the place. I can't remember who," she admitted. "I jumped at the chance to come back to Cattle Cove."

"Why was that?" Laney's voice was filled with compassion and not judgment.

She didn't dare look up at Ryan when she said, "This is the last place that felt like home to me in longer than I can remember."

Ryan excused himself and Alexis watched as he retraced the intruder's steps toward the tree line. For the first time since seeing him again, Rogue left her side to follow his master.

She figured he didn't need the sheriff breathing

down his neck about his choice to investigate the murders himself. His intentions were pretty clear, especially considering he'd just taken a picture of what would probably be called a suspect list.

As far as Ryan was concerned, she should've realized he and his family would want to conduct their own investigation. They were the kind of people who would take this very seriously, considering it had happened on their land.

The thought that someone Angel or Darcy knew could have tracked them down and murdered them sent another icy chill down Alexis's spine. It was unthinkable.

Alexis had pretty much kept to herself, so no long list of friends to interview on her side. Looking back, she'd done everything in her power to close herself off to everyone she cared about, including Ryan and his family. There was no massive trail of friends to investigate here or in Houston.

People seemed to like her and were friendly enough. She'd been closest with her mother, who, to be honest, had been more like a sister considering their ages were so close. And then there was Ryan, her best friend. Alexis had always liked having a couple of close friends rather than a roomful of people she knew on a surface level. She'd left being popular to others. Ryan, for example, with his athletic abilities always seemed to have people ready and willing to follow him wherever he went. It hadn't seemed to faze him one way or the other. He'd never gone to parties despite being invited.

She'd asked him why once and he'd just shrugged and said that it wasn't his scene. It was crazy to her how well he'd known himself at such a young age. She'd always wished that she'd had just a little bit of that self-confidence and sense of direction.

His compass seemed to have always pointed toward exactly where he'd ended up, his family's ranch. He'd always valued family over groupies, even though he'd had his fair share of those after a game. And walking away from college offers to play a sport he so clearly loved had always left her wondering why.

When she'd asked him about it, he'd simply said that he wanted to keep on loving it. If it was his job and he had pressure besides the kind he put on himself, he probably wouldn't enjoy it as much. And then he'd gone on about how his place was right there at the ranch, tending to the cattle and working on his family's legacy.

It was what he'd been born to do. The fact that he'd been born into a cattle ranching family just made it that much sweeter. Even if he hadn't and it hadn't been in his blood, she had no doubt that he would have found his way to one.

She, on the other hand, had had no such lightning strike about her future. She'd always dabbled in art and drawing. But the idea of creating art for a living scared her. She'd chalked it up to growing up without a security blanket and what little she'd had had been ripped out from underneath her.

When she'd thumbed through class descriptions at community college, she'd found a way to have a regular job and incorporate her art. Graphic design had looked like it would fit the bill and at least she got to be creative in her job. Although these days she did far more account management than art. She wouldn't be picky as long as she got the chance to be creative.

"Can you tell me about your co-worker?" the sheriff asked.

Alexis filled Sheriff Justice in on everything she knew, which could be summed up in ten minutes. It struck her just how little she knew the people she'd worked with. She updated the sheriff about Stevie and couldn't help but wonder if he was responsible.

"Which one of those vehicles is yours?" She nodded toward the pair of parked cars.

Alexis had driven her own car in case things didn't work out and she decided to leave early. She pointed to the blue compact sedan on the left of the small sport utility. The murderer must've guessed it belonged to Darcy.

"Mind if I walk over there and take a look at it?" Justice seemed to be fixated on something.

"Be my guest." Alexis shook her head. She rolled the cup of coffee in her palms, wishing for a refill. At least the caffeine had her brain waking up and clicking a little faster.

The sun was bright over the eastern horizon. She closed her eyes and leaned her head back against the headrest. She tried to let this whole scenario sink in. It was too much to take in all at once.

Piece by piece, she was beginning to digest the horrific events that had taken place. She looked up and let her gaze follow the sheriff who walked over to the vehicles and crouched down.

It was then that she realized that all of her tires had been slashed. So, great, she would need to call roadside assistance to change out her tires now or be stuck on the McGannon property.

Out of the corner of her eyes, she saw Ryan and Rogue walking back toward her. Again, she couldn't help but notice how striking he was. Ryan had always been good looking. He'd had such an easy charm about him that seemed gone now. His dark eyes were just as beautiful but more intense.

When he looked at her, it had felt like he could see right through her. It had been a long time since anyone had gotten past the smiling façade she usually put up. Most people took her at face value and moved on. Why wouldn't they? Not Ryan. He would take her aside and ask her what was wrong before she realized she might be frowning.

She'd learned to live with the past and had been determined to live her life. Even so, she couldn't help but notice how her mom had been struck down in her prime. After being a teenage mother and giving everything she'd had to Alexis, she was so close to living life for herself instead of for her child.

Not that Alexis wasn't grateful for the sacrifices. There wasn't a day in Alexis's childhood when she didn't feel loved and wanted. Not everybody got that, and she knew how very fortunate she was. And so, she'd learned to count her blessings.

"Is there anymore coffee?" She started to try to stand as Ryan and Rogue approached. Adrenaline had long since worn off and her ankle throbbed. Her head didn't feel much better. In fact, she couldn't decide what hurt worse. And yet she knew it could have turned out so much worse.

Ryan held his hand out. "I can take it and manage a refill."

"It's okay. You've already done enough. I know you're here for work anyway, so I don't want to be any more trouble than I have been." She wished she could reel those words in the minute they left her mouth based on his hurt expression. "I don't want you to think that I don't appreciate everything you've done."

"Is that the only reason you still think I'm here? Work reasons?" he asked. There was a storm raging behind those dark brown eyes.

"I'm sorry, Ryan. I just heard you say that you were here for work and—"

"I came out here because I didn't like the house being rented by strangers. So, yeah, I'm here for work. I'd be lying if I said that I wasn't here because of my job. But I'm here..." He pointed to the ground in front of her feet. "Because this involves someone I cared a lot about at one time. And that person, in case you were wondering, is you, Alexis."

He seemed like he was working up to say a whole lot more and then exhaled sharply. He looked like he was rethinking saying what was on his mind. And that was probably for the best. She didn't really need to know that he still cared about her. It wouldn't change anything.

After he took the cup from her hands, she folded her arms over her chest. "I wasn't trying to make you mad. I can't imagine doing any of this without a friend around."

He held up the coffee cup before turning to walk toward Hawk's pickup. "Good. Because I plan to stick around."

Her heart gave a traitorous little flip at the words.

RYAN BROUGHT fresh coffee to Alexis. Her eyes were still wild, and he needed to regroup so he could talk to her without letting his emotions take over. He reminded himself that he was no longer a teenager with rogue hormones that made him go from zero to over-the-top angry in the time it took start his car engine.

"I added a little more milk this time." He handed over the cup.

"It looks pretty perfect to me." She blinked at him with those pale blue eyes he could look into for days. She took a sip and then leaned her head back. She shut her eyes. "I'm sorry about what I said. Everything is so messed up, Ryan. This can't be happening. It doesn't feel real."

"No." He couldn't agree more. He took a long, hard look at her and saw that she was scared inside despite the strong front she put up. It was understandable under the circumstances and she needed to know that she didn't have to be so brave that she stuffed everything behind the wall and tried to deal with it all herself.

She opened her eyes and stared at the cabin. She was still in her pajamas despite mentioning she'd like to burn them. The sun might be up but she'd gotten up in the middle of the night. Or, at least, it would be for most. Ranchers routinely got up and to work around four a.m.

"Can I ask a personal question?" He wasn't sure how she'd take what he was about to offer. The last thing he wanted to do was offend her or make her hide behind more of those walls.

"Yeah." She didn't look at him. Instead, she stared into her cup of coffee and he saw her muscles tense ever so slightly like she was preparing for a punch.

Damn. He really felt like a jerk for not being a better friend to her years ago. But there was nothing stopping him from being one now.

"I'd like to get you out of here. What do you think about spending the rest of the day at my place? Maybe even stay over tonight. Just until you get your bearings."

"No, thanks." She didn't make eye contact. The rim of her cup got real interesting to her, though. "I'd better get home. I just want out of these clothes and to get my stuff back. I'll be okay."

At least she didn't lie and say that she was okay. Anyone could see that she wasn't. And he wouldn't expect her to be after what she'd gone through.

"You sure about that? Rogue here seems to have gotten pretty attached to you." His attempt at humor bombed but at least she reached down and scratched behind the dog's ears.

"He's a good boy," was all she said. Her mind seemed pretty made up.

"I understand if you have to get home to someone but I—"

"There's no one," she said quickly. Her cheeks flushed like they always did when she was embarrassed. She didn't have to be. It was just him, an old friend. An annoying voice tried to argue their relationship was more special to him than that, but he quashed it before it could take root in his mind. There was no use planting seeds that would never bear fruit.

"Then at least think about it." He had no plans to force her into anything but she needed to know that he was there for her. "It would give us a chance to catch up and..." He wasn't certain he should say the last part but decided to go for broke anyway. "I don't like the idea of you being on the road for hours by yourself and then going home alone after what just happened."

"I appreciate it, Ryan. I really do." There was so much sincerity in her words the knot that had formed in his gut tightened. "But the longer I put off being alone the harder it's going to get. I'm used to being on my own."

He could appreciate what she was saying but he worried she wasn't taking into consideration the fact that the shock would wear off.

But trying to force her wouldn't do any good. So, he came up with an alternative plan.

"I could follow you. Make sure you get home all right. Pick up dinner," he offered, taking a different tack.

"I'm blown away. I'm not sure what to say to that. It's a really nice offer—"

Before she could come up with a reason to push him away again, he held his hand up. "Then, don't overthink it. Take me up on it."

"I don't know. It's asking a lot to have you drive all the way to Houston only to come back tonight."

"Well, that's the great part. I don't mind."

She bit down on her bottom lip, a sure sign she was thinking about it at least. Her forehead creased, the lines deepening.

"It's not a good idea," she started to protest, but he wasn't letting her get off that easy.

"Which is exactly why we should do it." He could only hope she remembered those sentences were the start of many of their adventures.

6

R yan was making it next to impossible to turn down his offer. He'd made a point of using a phrase from their past and it hadn't gotten past her. Alexis took another sip of her coffee, mainly to stall for time. Part of her wanted nothing more than to stay at his place or have him come to hers.

The thought of going home alone sent a shiver down her spine. Being in Ryan's general vicinity was like standing next to the sun. She could soak up all the warmth...but then what? Step back into the harsh cold? What would that be like? She'd been forced to walk away from Ryan McGannon once and she still had the frostbite to prove it.

This time, she was more prepared. This time, she wouldn't get close enough to feel the loss because it had almost shattered her to walk away from everything she knew before. This time, she'd be smarter.

"I'll think about it, Ryan. But let's be honest. You're needed here at the ranch—"

As if on cue, his cell buzzed and she was grateful for the interruption. Turning him down was going to be harder than she realized. It didn't help that his McGannon charm was on full force. The dimple that peeked out when he smiled caused her heart to stir in ways she couldn't afford.

He excused himself and turned toward the tree line. Another shiver raced down her spine at the realization her assailant had disappeared in the same direction. Her pulse kicked up at the thought he might still be out there somewhere watching. Waiting.

If it hadn't been so dark earlier, she might have been able to get a description of him. As it was, he could walk right by her and she wouldn't know him from Adam.

Suddenly, the suggestion of heading indoors sounded better than it had a few minutes ago. There was no way she was going back inside that cabin, or indeed any other cabin for the rest of her life, if she had anything to say about it.

An eerie feeling crept over her. It was most likely her imagination working overtime, but she had the distinct feeling that someone actually was watching her. People described the sensation as a cat walking over their grave.

She looked around, surveying the area. There was no way the guy would come back. Right? That would just be foolish or reckless. She'd read news stories about killers joining search parties for victims for the sick pleasure of feeling like they were getting one over on people. Or to stay close to the investigation. She couldn't even begin to fathom the kind of twisted mind it would take for someone to do that.

Refocusing her attention, she couldn't help but overhear Ryan's conversation.

"So there's still no change?" he asked.

He was quiet for a few seconds. He stood in an athletic stance like he was bracing himself for bad news. His left hand was fisted and planted on his hip. He looked out onto the same tree line she had moments ago.

"Has the doctor made any predictions as to when he might regain consciousness?"

Her heart sank at the possibility that something might have happened to one of his brothers or cousins. His family had always been close and had always accepted her as one of their own since she and Ryan were friends. Then there was his dad, who had been nothing but kind to her.

"Okay. Thanks for the update. I appreciate it." Ryan paused. "If anything changes..." His voice trailed off and she could hear a hint of sadness in his tone. Not a moment later, he ended the call.

He stood there for a long moment before issuing a

sharp breath and turning to face her. Pain was detailed in his dark features but he seemed to get a grip when he took in his second breath.

"Is everything okay at home?" She still cared about the McGannons even though she'd lost touch with them. Ryan's serious expression was too hard to read. Frustrated? Sad?

Not being able to tell what he was thinking reminded her of what had been lost between them as friends. There was a time when one look was all it took to be able tell what the other was thinking.

A piece of her missed having that kind of bond with someone...with him.

"It's Dad. He took a fall in the equipment building where we keep a lot of the farming equipment. He must've taken a blow to his head when he fell because he lost consciousness and has been in a coma ever since." There was so much anguish in his eyes when he spoke.

"Oh, Ryan. I'm so sorry. Your Dad is...was...always so kind to me. I hope everything turns out all right." Her heart went out to him.

"I appreciate it."

"Was he alone? Does anyone know how it happened?" she asked.

"Uncle Donny was with him." He shot her a look. "He was in the building and somehow missed it all. Said he asked Dad a question and when he got no response he went back to work. A little while later he asked again and decided to walk across the building in case Dad couldn't hear. Apparently, Dad had music playing and Uncle Donny said that's the reason he didn't hear the fall. He immediately called 9-1-1, and said Dad was just lying there knocked out."

She studied him. There was something that he wasn't telling her. "You're not buying his excuse, are you?"

"I have questions."

"Like what?" She hated that anything had happened to such a nice man.

"Levi had our attorney pull up Dad's will, just to make sure there hadn't been any changes since Uncle Donny came back. He's trouble, the kind of person who you just know something bad is going to happen around, but you can't exactly pinpoint the reason why. Trouble seems to follow him but also rolls off of him and impacts those around him the most," he explained.

"Like this kind of trouble?" She nodded toward the cabin.

"I don't think he'd have anything to gain. I have personal knowledge he's been trying to wrangle more power in the family business, though."

"What's he even doing here?" She figured it couldn't be for family reasons.

"It's not for his sons. He couldn't care less about them despite putting on a show every time the family gathers for a holiday. Levi hardly comes around the big house because the whole situation frustrates him."

"I thought your uncle asked your father to cash out his interest in the cattle ranch forever ago. I don't ever remember him coming around at all when we were in high school." She didn't have any personal knowledge of the man.

"He wasn't anywhere in sight while he had money. According to Levi, our uncle went through his inheritance because he overheard him talking to our dad basically begging for more."

"How on earth did he go through that much money?" She had never really spoken to Ryan about his family's money, but it had to be more than she could imagine. He was and had always been one of the most down-to-earth people she'd ever met. He was grounded in a rare way that made him relatable despite the trust fund he must have waiting for him.

She'd only been aware of his family's wealth in the times they'd gone into town. Shop owners treated him like royalty even though it had seemed to embarrass him. Between his family's money and his celebrity baseball status, he was quite popular. She'd realized that he was in a class by himself by the way others had treated him.

"The best my brothers and I can tell he gambled it all away. You know our father. He wouldn't say an unkind word about another soul. He just wasn't built that way. And anyone who came to him in need wouldn't be turned down; he'd find a job for them or give them advice on how to get back on their feet." It was true. She'd heard Clive McGannon's reputation. She would almost swear that he was the one who'd arranged for her to stay in the bed and breakfast in town for the rest of her senior year free of charge. Although, it had never been confirmed. Granted, he would have wanted to keep his involvement under the radar, but she was pretty certain he'd been the one responsible. At the time, she'd been too broken to think it through. Now, she wanted to circle back and find a way to thank him.

"But that had to have been millions." She couldn't fathom that kind of money.

Ryan shrugged. "I guess when it comes to Uncle Donny it's an easy come, easy go situation. As kind as my father was, I don't think he would've allowed his brother back on the ranch if it wasn't for my cousins. Knowing Dad, he would want their father to be around despite the fact that Dad was the one who'd raised them, not Uncle Donny."

"Far be it from me to sit as judge and jury on anyone else's life. I'm far from perfect. But what kind of person asks to be bought out of a family legacy and then blows the money in a manner of...what years? A decade?" She looked up and caught his intense gaze.

"The worst part was that once his bank account was full, he had no problem taking off and leaving his boys in my dad's care. Don't get me wrong, we loved

having all of us under one roof. We were a handful
though, and a lot to keep up with." His face broke into
a slight smile at the memory.

"I remember how rowdy you guys could be outside.
But that never spilled over into the house. Everyone's
boots ended up in a neat line on the back porch. Not a
toe out of place."

"Penny ran a tight ship." He chuckled and she was
grateful to be able to break up some of the tension and
bring a smile to his face despite the fact it faded far too
quickly.

She told herself it was to thank his father but found
herself wanting to stick around during his recovery. A
little voice in the back of her mind called her out on
the lie.

Being around Ryan felt a little too good and a little
too right. And for a second, she didn't want to overthink her next words.

"If your offer still stands, I'd like to come back to
the big house with you."

RYAN COULDN'T HIDE his surprise at the about-face.
Rather than ask what changed her mind, he nodded.
He wanted to get her out of there and he needed a
chance to go over the evidence.

"Let's go."

He held out a hand, which she took, and he

ignored the frisson of heat traveling up his arm from the point of contact. The heat that he'd felt between them reawakened. As a teen, and someone who was supposed to be her friend, he hadn't wanted to acknowledge the chemistry between them. Hell, he'd never felt anything so strong in his life.

If he was being real honest, he still hadn't. Seeing her again reminded him of the fact. As a grown man, he would know exactly what to do with an attraction as strong as the one he felt toward Alexis.

But this was his best friend. She'd jumped ship on him once and if he had anything to say about it, they'd stay in contact this time. Rogue moved to the side as he helped her out of the SUV.

Tuck was taking pictures of the ground around the porch. Ryan waved at him, catching his attention.

"I'm taking her to the big house. If you have any other questions for her, she'll be with me for the rest of the day." He glanced at Alexis for confirmation and she nodded.

His traitorous heart gave another squeeze when she agreed to come home with him. The look on her face—even though it was just a flash—that said she felt safe with him stirred up interesting emotions. Having her back in his life, even for a fleeting moment, reminded him of how good life had been with her in it.

Tuck waved them on.

"Any chance he'll bring me my clothes?" She glanced down at her pajamas.

"If not, I'll find something you can use at the house." He took a few steps toward Tuck and asked if she could have any of her belongings.

"The cabin hasn't been cleared yet. I'm sorry," he said.

She wouldn't get very far without her purse, keys or license.

"Do you want to lean more of your weight on me?" Making eye contact was a mistake he wouldn't make twice while he stood this close. Because he recognized need when it passed behind her baby blues, and it took all his willpower not to act on it.

"Okay," she said and her voice was low and gravelly. If he didn't know better, he'd mistake it for more of that desire he'd seen in her eyes.

Hell, McGannon, he was most likely imagining things. His mind was playing tricks on him to break up some of the tension of the heavy morning.

"He slit my tires, Ryan."

"I'll get them taken care of as soon as we get clearance." His promise was met with a nod. "Hawk can hang around here until they're finished inside the house. I'll ask him to bring your belongings up to the big house. This crew will most likely be working here for a while."

She heaved another sigh and bit down on her bottom lip. He'd noticed the tick years ago and it always made him want to reach out to comfort her.

Rogue followed them to Hawk's work truck. The

keys were inside. It was unusual to lock doors in Cattle Cove until recently. He helped Alexis into the passenger side and then fired off a text to let Hawk know he was taking the truck. His own vehicle was about half a mile up the road. Hawk said he didn't mind taking it back to the big house later.

After making sure Alexis was comfortable, he claimed the driver's seat and called for Rogue to hop in. He did, and then positioned himself in the middle of the bench seat.

"You're probably starving by now." Ryan patted the dog's head.

Ears forward, tongue wagging, Rogue had settled down considerably since this morning. He'd caught the scent of the perp and with his keen hearing might have heard Alexis. This guy deserved one helluva treat. His quick actions most likely saved Alexis's life.

Ryan started the engine and put the gearshift in reverse. He didn't want to think about what might have happened if Rogue hadn't gotten there in time.

Keeping inside the property, the usual twenty-five-minute drive took less than twenty. He wanted to get her out of those clothes and into something more comfortable. The way she kept fidgeting and picking at the shirt told him just how uncomfortable she was.

He wouldn't mind changing his clothes and tossing his current outfit on top of a fire, either. He'd always remember the victims if he ever wore this shirt and jeans again. Time to chunk them in the trash.

With the cabin being a rental, it might be difficult to separate out any DNA evidence. He wanted to take a look at the rental log for the past few weeks and see if there was any crossover with the names Alexis had supplied on the notepad.

He parked in the lot next to the big house. Rogue jumped out right behind him. He made it around the truck and to the passenger side as Alexis tried to hobble out.

"You can lean on me," he offered.

She did, and more of that heat pulsed through him, warming places that had been iced over far too long. Rather than get inside his head about why his former best friend was causing a reaction from him, he helped her inside the back door.

Ryan couldn't help but smile as he noticed the perfectly straight line of boots she'd joked about. He toed his off and tossed them inside the trash.

"I thought it would be strange to come back here," Alexis said. "But it feels a lot like home."

7

"You're welcome here anytime, Alexis."

Alexis wasn't sure why she'd blurted out her feelings about being back at the big house. Embarrassment heated her cheeks.

"Thank you." She turned her face away from him to hide the red blush creeping up her neck.

"I'm serious. I don't like the circumstances one bit, but I can't deny that it's good to see you again." His voice had deepened over the years and was like smooth whiskey as it traveled over her skin. "The way we left things before..."

She cleared her throat to ease the sudden dryness. Her mind blanked out on her, failing to give her words. She wanted to tell him that she was sorry for walking away and not looking back, but her mouth clamped shut. Her pulse sped up and her chest squeezed. *Air*, she needed to breathe. Now. Her lungs failed. Her palms were suddenly damp, and a cold sweat swept over her.

Before she could figure out her next words, Penny walked into the room, breaking the tension that was building between them. "I heard what happened from Hawk. I'm sorry about your friends, Alexis."

Alexis had no idea of Penny's age and wouldn't be caught dead asking. The older woman could best be described at tiny but mighty, maybe in her mid- to late-sixties. Her frame might be petite, but she has a natural skip to her step that made her seem taller. She had on what she usually wore, a blouse with jeans. And her favorite apron still hung on a hook in the kitchen. It read: BOSS. Her salt and pepper hair was styled short and feathered to one side. But it was Penny's clear green eyes that were the most striking feature.

The older woman walked right over and brought Alexis into an embrace. Penny had been a mother figure to Ryan, his brothers and their cousins. She'd been like a second mother to Alexis.

A tidal wave of emotion descended, threatening to pull her under. She held tight to Penny as memories crushed down on her. So many happy memories of Friday nights spent at the ranch after school. Her and Ryan rode horses and took walks. They'd stay out late, lie on a blanket, and stare up at the stars.

Texas had the most amazingly vast and open sky that seemed like it went on forever. A dark canopy only made the twinkling stars more brilliant. She couldn't count the number of times she'd sat outside on the bench on a Sunday afternoon watching Ryan pitch with one of his brothers on the diamond his father had built after watching one of his son's games.

She and Ryan would talk for hours about the pressure he felt to be a baseball player despite a lack of desire to do it for a living. He'd been good at it because he loved it. That didn't mean he wanted to play for a living. She'd loved that her friend had known himself so well.

The day he'd told his father about his plans to work the ranch instead of accept one of many offers on the table, he'd asked her to be waiting for him in case he needed moral support.

They'd stayed out past curfew that night and she'd gotten busted by her mom, who'd come home halfway through her shift when she couldn't reach Alexis. Getting grounded had been worth it, though.

It had been one of the best nights of her young life. Alexis had no idea how much her life was about to change or how much she was about to lose. She shook off the revelry before it held her under water until she could no longer breathe.

Pulling back, she said, "It's really good to see you again, Miss Penny."

The older woman's gaze bounced from Alexis to Ryan and back. "Same to you, Alexis. Have you eaten anything today?"

"No, ma'am." Before she could protest, Penny was on her way to the fridge.

"I'll grab a change of clothes," Ryan said after helping Alexis to the large hand-carved table that took up one side of the room. Out of the corner of her eye, she watched as Ryan fed Rogue before disappearing down the hallway.

She'd been in this house so many times and not much had changed. It was still as big and still as beautiful as she remembered. The place had a pull up a chair and talk for a while feeling.

"Can I get you some water or coffee?" Penny asked.

"Both if it's no trouble but I can get them. I remember where they are." Her last two cups of coffee had gone cold before she'd had a chance to finish them.

Penny waved her off and made a pfff sound. "You sit there and put that ankle up."

Actually, that was a great idea. It would probably help with the swelling.

Penny padded over to the coffee maker and poured a cup. "Do you still take milk?"

"Yes, ma'am."

"All right then." Penny fixed up the coffee and brought over a glass of water.

By the time Alexis took the first sip, Ryan returned with a stack of folded clothes. She noticed that he'd already changed and was carrying clothes in a trash bag. The reality that her friends were dead struck like a bullet.

With Ryan's help, she made it to the downstairs bathroom.

"Will you wait for me?" she asked.

"Yes." Something that looked a lot like need darkened behind his eyes as he took a step back, crossed his arms over his chest and leaned against the wall. They'd never been romantically involved as teens despite feeling a draw toward Ryan that was so much more than friends. No *friend* she'd ever known made her skin sizzle wherever they touched.

Getting out of her pajamas made her start to feel human again. She picked up the clothing that Ryan left on the counter and smiled. Her old yoga pants and workout bra with her favorite tank. The clothes were from high school and fit a little snug, but she managed all right.

She'd just about worn the lotus flower tank to threads and it was as soft as she remembered it to be. She opened the door and leaned on the sink to stabilize herself.

One look at her and Ryan cleared his throat. A small smile tugged at the corners of his mouth—a mouth she had no business staring at.

"You became exactly what you wanted, Ryan. I'm really proud of you," she said.

"Yeah," was all he said. She wanted to know more about what he'd been up to for the past dozen years but figured she had no right to ask. He was down to one-word answers and she wondered if he regretted helping her.

Then, she remembered about his father and wondered how much of the storm brewing behind Ryan's eyes had to do with his dad's situation. She gathered up her clothes and tossed them inside the plastic trash bag, joining his.

She leaned on him on the way back to the kitchen and neither spoke. Her stomach growled despite thinking there was no way she could eat a bite.

Ryan joined her at the table where a fresh cup of coffee waited for him. He thanked Penny and updated her on the no-news about his father.

"I'm planning to head over to the hospital. Hawk was going to take me this morning but..." She flashed apologetic eyes at Alexis on her way to bring a pair of full plates over. She sat them down in front of Alexis and Ryan. But there was something in her voice that was different when she mentioned Hawk. The two went way back and it was probably mutual concern for their friend and employer.

"Thank you," they both echoed and it was a blast from the past.

Penny had made the works. Eggs, bacon, hash browns. And despite feeling nauseated, she cleaned her plate. Pain killers always made her a little bit sick to her stomach and she probably needed the food to absorb the pill she'd taken last night.

Last night suddenly felt like a lifetime ago. Yesterday seemed like an alternate universe. At least Alexis was out of those clothes she'd had on. She felt a little bit more like her old self in her outfit. She remembered the rubber band she always kept around her wrist and pulled her hair off her face, tying it up.

"Are you guys all right here?" Penny asked.

Alexis bit back a yawn as she nodded. She took a sip of coffee to shake off the tiredness trying to take over. She realized she'd gotten to bed last night after midnight and was awake before the sun.

"The food was amazing. Thank you." She also remembered how amazing Penny's cooking was.

"It's no trouble." Penny waved the compliment off like it was nothing. After living on her own and not being so great in the kitchen, Alexis could really appreciate a good meal. She'd gotten the no-cooking gene from her mother, who could barely boil water without catching something on fire.

Being back in Cattle Cove made Alexis feel closer to her mother. She stared at the rim of her coffee cup. Had she blocked out the good memories of her along with the overwhelming sense of loss?

"Are you heading to the hospital?" Ryan asked Penny.

"Ensley said she'd swing by the house and pick me up." She twisted her hands together.

"Ensley Cartier?" Alexis asked under her breath. "She's back in town?"

which meant she had less than six hours of sleep after being in the sun all day.

Looking at her, he didn't want to disturb her. The bed in the guest room would be a helluva lot more comfortable. There was one down the hall on the first floor that he figured he could get her to without much protest.

He smiled at the empty cup of coffee. Not even a fresh cup of caffeine could keep her eyes open.

"Come on." After setting the printout down, he helped her to standing before walking her the short distance to the guest bedroom. The place was always made up because Penny liked to be prepared.

He pulled the comforter down and helped her climb inside the sheets. The way she looked up at him with those sleepy eyes tugged at his heart.

"Lay down with me until I go back to sleep?" she said on a yawn.

It was probably a bad idea but, hell, he was all-in at this point. He climbed in next to her, and she curled her warm body against him. She pulled off the rubber band holding her hair in a ponytail, and her silky blond threads spilled out over his arm and across the pillow.

Damned if his heart didn't take another hit.

Rogue hopped up onto the foot of the bed and made himself comfortable. Despite only planning to stay in the guest room for a few minutes, Ryan closed his eyes and fell asleep.

He woke an hour later thinking that Alexis felt a little too right in his arms. Her soft skin and curvy body was curled around him, molding perfectly to him. He couldn't help but notice how perfectly the two of them fit.

At some point in the last hour, Rogue had repositioned so that he was right in the mix.

Ryan leaned over, pressing a kiss to Alexis's cheek. She released a little moan of pleasure as she stretched out her body beside him. His arm was still around her neck. His body reminded him how beautiful she was by his blood flooding south and giving him a painfully stiff erection.

As far as playing it cool went, he was losing big time.

8

Alexis woke with a start. She felt around the bed, searching for Ryan but found cold sheets where he used to be. She tried to move, and her body screamed. Her ankle wasn't having any of it.

She sat up, trying to get her bearings. Rogue was curled up at her feet on the bed. It was dark inside the room thanks to blinds and heavy curtains but the clock on the nightstand read three thirty in the afternoon. This time of year, the sun would be up for hours.

The bed was soft. She propped up a couple of pillows behind her back and head to make herself more comfortable. She'd slept in this room a handful of times over the years when her mother was going to visit her fiancé for the weekend.

She still remembered the look on her mother's face when she asked if she could sleep over her best friend's house. Her mother had responded that she thought Ryan was Alexis's best friend.

Alexis had smiled and said that he was, and he was. There'd been a few times when they'd looked at each other back then and she could've sworn there was something more going on between them. But she hadn't wanted to ruin their friendship.

The McGannon ranch had been like a second home. She glanced over at the nightstand again and it took a second to register that her phone was with the sheriff. She usually kept it plugged in next to the bed.

Leaning her head back, she tried to force the memory of her attacker's face and came up short. If only she could have gotten a better look at him. She fisted her hands. Rogue stood up, like he sensed her mood shift.

"Sorry, buddy. I'm just frustrated." Having him around gave her a sense of security. Maybe it was time to get a dog of her own. She leaned forward and scratched behind his ears. "You're a good dog."

She highly doubted Ryan would give up his near-constant companion to make her feel comforted. But maybe he could hook her up with a pet like Rogue.

Alexis peeled back the covers and took a look at her ankle. It was still a little swollen and bruised but it was healing. She wanted to circle back with Sheriff Justice to see if there were any leads.

As much as she loved being back at the ranch, she also needed to think about heading home at some point. Her car. More of that frustration surfaced. A shudder rocked her body at the fact that the murderer had been trying to ensure no one got away.

His words came back to mind and the chilling sound of his voice. *You aren't supposed to be here.*

At first, she'd taken the comment at first value like she'd surprised him by being downstairs when she was supposed to be asleep in the loft. What if it meant something else? What if it meant that he was surprised by a third person being at the cabin?

That lead her to believe his actions were premeditated and that he was possibly someone who had access to the reservations system at the ranch. Who would that be? Definitely not a McGannon.

Another possibility was Darcy's ex. The sheriff would be able to get a description of him from Darcy's parents. With her being a college student in Austin at a major university it might be difficult to track down her friends without phone numbers. Alexis could look at Darcy's social media accounts but people her age usually had hundreds if not thousands of online followers or friends. Darcy didn't work, so going to her job wasn't an option. There was no way Alexis would show up at the Pruitt family home. Law enforcement would do that and deliver horrific news. There was no reason to add to their pain.

There was also a possibility this was a random attack and had nothing to do with anyone they were acquainted with. Although the attacker's chilling words, words that she couldn't quite shake, made her think otherwise.

Would a random person watch the place and then wait for an opportunity? Come back at night after gathering intel? If so, then wouldn't he know there were three people in the cabin?

There'd been two vehicles parked outside. She guessed it was possible he believed each person inside drove themselves. But a person who'd been watching them would have seen all three of them together on the back porch that overlooked the lake.

Again, the thought of being watched creeped her out. Alexis hoped they'd get answers soon. The thought that this bastard could hurt someone else sent anger shooting through her as she climbed off the side of the bed and tested her ankle. It screamed pretty hard at her but she could make it to the bathroom on her own.

She hop-walked into the adjoining room with Rogue a step behind. Time might have passed but very little had changed in the guest room area. Other than updating the comforter and curtains in the bedroom, little had changed there, as well.

The bathroom was large and stocked. She moved to the sink and found all the supplies she'd hoped would be there. After washing her face and brushing her teeth she felt a little bit more human. She grabbed the rubber band from her wrist and pulled her hair back from her face in a ponytail.

Rogue sat next to her leg. If he kept this up, she was going to have some hard negotiating ahead of her to take him away from Ryan. It was easy to see how much the two adored each other. Her work would be cut out for her to say the least.

Her new friend followed her as she made her way down the hallway and into the kitchen. She half expected Ryan to be there and was surprised when he wasn't.

Voices drifted from down the hall and she realized someone was with him in the living room. A quick glance down at her outfit and she figured this was as good as it was going to get today. Everything was covered, even if the yoga pants were a little more snug now than they had been in high school.

She hobbled her way toward the sound of the voices and recognized Tuck's along with Ryan's.

On the coffee table in front of them, Ryan had several pieces of paper fanned out. Elbows on his thighs, he was bent forward and pointing at one of the papers. She cleared her throat so they would know she was there.

Both men immediately stood.

"I woke up a few minutes ago and decided to see where you went." Her gaze was intent on Ryan. There was something about his calm presence that kept her stress levels below panic. She'd chalk it up to their history, and that was probably partly true, but there was just something about how grounded he was that centered her in a way she'd never known with anyone else.

A long friendship had a way of doing that, she figured. She regretted denying herself that for so long. In Houston, she'd always worked long hours or studied. She'd told herself that was the reason she didn't have a long list of friends.

A truth hit her square in the chest. She'd closed herself off to the world. It had been a really long time since she'd let anyone get close to her.

"Tuck and I were just talking about the case," Ryan motioned for her to come sit with them. He locked gazes with her. "Do you need a hand?"

"No, I'm good. Thanks, though." It was important for her to be able to do things for herself and especially after what had happened. Walking across the room might seem insignificant to some but doing it on her own, unaided, was important to her. She might have been knocked off balance last night, but she rebounded. She could sleep in her own bed and not be too scared to turn off the lights.

She walked to the chair opposite the men and took a seat. They brought her up to speed with the theories they'd been working on and they were right on track with hers; Darcy's ex-boyfriend, a past renter, or a passerby who'd been watching the cabin.

"Everyone on the ranch will be investigated, including me and our roster of ranch hands, but it's only to dot every I and cross every T." Ryan clasped his hands together. "It's unlikely we'll uncover anything going on around here. Although, with Dad's condition under investigation, there's something in the air."

Her mind immediately snapped to Ryan's uncle. "How tall is Donny?"

"He's on the short side for our family. Maybe six-feet tall with shoes on. I can show you a picture of him if you think it'll help," Ryan offered.

Alexis nodded her head. Ryan was to his feet and crossing the room to the mantel where several framed pictures lined the wood above the stone fireplace. The big house lived up to its name. All the rooms were a good size. This room alone would take up Alexis and her mother's apartment over the Dover's garage. It was meant for a mother-in-law, but they'd rented it out to Alexis and her mother for years.

Her mother had liked the fact that the elderly couple was close by in case Alexis needed anything. Working the nightshift made her worry about her only daughter. Maybe a little too much, but Alexis had always prided herself on being able to take care of herself. She'd probably taken it to a fault since losing her mother. This trip had opened her eyes to just how much she'd shut the door on her past and closed herself off to new relationships.

That needed to change. Work should lighten up now that her boss's sister-in-law could be around to pitch in. His wife had gotten through the worst of her treatments and was starting to come through the other side. Life was looking up.

Or at least it had been until last night.

RYAN WATCHED Alexis for a reaction as he handed her the photo frame of Uncle Donny. He'd intentionally given her one of the whole family that had been taken last Christmas, minus Levi, so she had a basis for comparison.

She studied the man in the picture before shaking her head. "I'm positive it's not him."

Her response wasn't all that unexpected. Ryan didn't hold his uncle in high esteem, but he seriously doubted the man would murder two innocent women, especially so close to home.

But would he look the other way if his brother slipped and fell, hoping to step in and take over the ranch? That was unnervingly possible.

Even Uncle Donny had to know the family wouldn't easily step aside and allow that to happen. Of course, he wouldn't come at them directly. He'd figure out a way through a backdoor, find a loophole that allowed him to take control over the place.

Levi had been clear with his thoughts on the subject and Ryan couldn't agree more. Uncle Donny would take over the ranch over their dead bodies.

"Sheriff Justice called Houston P.D. An officer notified the Pruitts of their loss." Tuck had already told Ryan.

Alexis took a moment of silence before she spoke. "Did they send over a description of Darcy's ex-boyfriend by any chance?"

"The Pruitts said he's tall and used to play high school football. Said he has more of a runner's build," Tuck informed.

"The guy I remember was thick." She brought her hands out, palms facing each other. "He covered the doorframe."

"You said you didn't get a good look at his facial features."

She shook her head. "No. It was too dark in the hallway."

It was possible, and especially considering that she'd been on medication, that her mind had played a trick on her. Or he might have had on layers that made him look bigger than he was. The height matched her description but not his thickness.

"She talked about how possessive he'd become. He didn't want her going to parties without him. She had to sneak out to see friends in the last few weeks of their relationship. He said a few things to her that didn't sit well after the breakup. Darcy took in all in stride, saying she'd hurt him by being the one to end it. Angel had stronger feelings about the whole situation." She leaned forward and rubbed her temples.

"Doesn't sound like her sister liked Stevie," Tuck observed.

"Her feelings for him were a lot stronger than that. Darcy stopped Angel from going into detail but I got the impression he'd been physical with her at some point in the relationship. Based on what Darcy said yesterday his temper was the reason she finally decided to break it off. She also reminded her sister the relationship was over and that it wouldn't do any good to keep rehashing it. Darcy was done with him." Alexis reached down and absently stroked Rogue's fur.

The dog had found a new best friend, which was odd because he generally didn't take to new people. He was a friendly enough animal, but he usually kept a distance, assessing a person before he got too close. Maybe it was the trauma she'd been through or that Ryan had accepted her so easily, but Rogue stayed practically glued to her side.

Ryan's chest swelled a little more because he liked that Rogue had accepted her as one of the pack.

"Stevie Patterson has a history of violence with women," Tuck informed. "His last girlfriend took out a restraining order on him. The violence seemed to be escalating and she told the court she was beginning to fear for her life."

Too bad he didn't match the description of the man Alexis had encountered. Everything about him seemed to fit the profile. Darcy had ended the relationship after it got too heated. Stevie Patterson wasn't having it. He decided that if he couldn't have her no one could.

Ryan's grip tightened around the frame as he walked over to the fireplace and placed the photo in its spot. His hand fisted.

The murders didn't seem to fit a random killer profile. Smothering the life out of someone required getting up close and personal. It also meant he'd been methodical. He'd killed Darcy first and then Angel.

And then what? Had he planned to go upstairs or didn't he realize Alexis was there?

Ryan couldn't help but think the order of the deaths might be an important point to take note of. Granted, the guy might've levered the front door open and Darcy was right there, a victim of opportunity.

Or maybe Stevie was the murderer and he wanted to make damn sure she was dead first.

All Ryan knew for certain was that they were looking for a big man with a large frame who owned or had access to a dirt bike. Since his brother A.J. was managing the rental, he needed to get him in on this conversation.

Normally, his brothers and cousins would be coming and going. Life had been turned upside down since their father's so-called accident. He texted A.J. to come to the big house as soon as he was available.

The response came right away.

I'll be right there.

9

A.J. was a McGannon to a T. Tall and broad, with muscles for days. He had the carved from granite jawline like his brothers and cousins, and the hawk-like nose of his father. He was almost as good looking as Ryan, in Alexis's opinion. Almost.

There'd always been something extra hot about Ryan. Despite being friends, she'd always known he was more tempting than a hot fudge sundae seven days into a diet. In high school, she'd just never seen him as boyfriend material. Then again, they'd been friends and there was no way she would've ruined it with a fling.

Ryan never got too attached to a girlfriend and there'd always been plenty waiting in line whenever he wanted a date. He'd never had to work hard at it. He'd date someone for a little while and then move on.

Once or twice, when he'd been in between girl-friends, she thought she'd picked up on something happening between the two of them. Neither one of them had acted on it. Both seemed content to keep their friendship and it was probably for the best.

Or was it? a little voice in the back of her mind questioned. Walking away from Ryan and Cattle Cove had nearly gutted her.

"Thanks for coming on such short notice." Ryan walked across the room and gave his brother a hug. Alexis had always loved witnessing their family bond. There were a lot of McGannons and they all had distinct personalities. But when it came to having each other's backs there was no question. Pick on one and it was picking on them all.

A.J. acknowledged Tuck before his gaze landed on Alexis.

"It's good to see you around this place again," was all he said but those words seemed loaded. She was just beginning to see how much she might have hurt Ryan and his brothers by turning her back on the town.

"Sorry about the circumstances," she said but he shook his head.

"Not your fault."

Alexis took in a breath and nodded. She knew, on some level, that she wasn't responsible for Darcy and Angel's murders and yet she couldn't help but feel the weight of an unspoken burden. She couldn't help but wonder why she was still alive when they were gone. She'd had similar feelings when her mother died.

Survivor's guilt. That's the term her counselor had thrown out.

She'd looked up the term online and could check a few of the boxes. She felt numb after losing her mother. She had difficulty sleeping. There were so many times when she thought her mother would walk through the door while Alexis was still in bed. Her mother would sit at the foot of Alexis's bed and talk quietly about her shift.

The memory caused Alexis's chest to squeeze. It suddenly felt like the air had been sucked out of the room and her lungs were closing in. She reminded herself to breathe, refusing to let panic set in. She flexed and released her fingers to ease some of the tension in her body.

Focusing on Ryan, who seemed to realize she was going under, helped keep her afloat. He locked gazes and a moment happened between them. In those few seconds, if felt like the past decade plus disappeared. Time stopped. They were teenagers again with their whole lives ahead of them. Their biggest problems were how to spend the weekend, or how long they should study for a Lit exam. Shakespeare had never been her favorite.

A few more breaths and she picked up on the conversation thread happening between Tuck and A.J. while he opened the laptop he'd brought. No doubt, he was planning to pull up all the registrations in recent months.

"I think we should look for lone renters," Tuck said. "Anyone who might have rented the cabin under the guise of a fishing trip."

"We've had a few of those. Not many," A.J. supplied as his fingers danced on the keyboard. "Is there a description I should be looking for?"

"Does someone meet the renters?" Tuck asked.

"I do sometimes. For others I leave the key under the mat. A lot depends on when a person is getting in and what their needs are."

"How do you know who you're renting to?" Good question.

"I always ask for a copy of their driver's license to keep on file." A.J. pulled up the rental files on his laptop and turned the screen to face Tuck. "I can pull up the pictures one by one."

"Okay." Tuck leaned forward. "If we get any hits on the description, we can have Alexis take a look. No use wasting her time viewing anyone we can rule out ourselves."

"Your friend rented the cabin, right?" A.J. asked.

"Yes."

"I only show two guests on the file," he said.

"Oh, right. I came onboard last minute." She'd forgotten about that. "I joked that I got invited to help keep the cost down. Angel laughed and said she didn't mind that part. We'd been talking more in the break room lately and she thought her sister needed to be around another grown woman who *had her shit together*."

"Did Angel say how she found us?" A.J.'s question was a reasonable one.

"Someone at the office recommended this place. I'm not sure who she talked to. She handled all the finances for campaigns and worked pretty closely with quite a few of our clients to help them set realistic budgets. She might have mentioned a name, but it didn't stick." Alexis thought back and reached for discussion she'd had with Angel. Nothing came up. "I told her that I couldn't come at first. A couple of days later she showed me a picture of the cabin and I recognized it. I told her that I needed the break and that I was familiar with the ranch."

Tuck made a few notes and A.J. rocked his head.

"That explains why your name isn't on file," he said.

Alexis most likely wouldn't have changed her mind about going if she'd had to give her name. Being back on McGannon land was one thing. The family knowing she was there was something altogether different. The thought of running into Ryan and finding out he had a wife and kids had struck hard. She'd tried to reason her emotions away, telling herself that she only cared because it would be weird for him to be so grown up. And yet, a piece of her wanted to believe that he was still single.

Moving away from home was strange. Part of her had expected the place and everyone in it to be exactly the way it was when she'd left.

People said it was impossible to go home again and she finally realized how true that statement was because time stopped for no one.

"We'll take a look here and see what we can find. We'll let you know if there's anything worth looking at." A.J. would respect his renter's privacy.

"Do you want to grab a cup of coffee or something to eat in the kitchen?" Ryan seemed to take the cue.

"I should probably keep something in my stomach. The painkiller usually makes me queasy if I don't eat."

Ryan offered his arm and she took it. She also noticed what looked like an approving glance from A.J. and she had to stop herself from telling him she was only there for the day. In fact, she needed to think about going home soon.

"Is there any word on my car?" she asked Ryan as soon as they were out of earshot.

"Are you in a hurry to leave?" There was an undercurrent of hurt in his voice.

"I can't stay here forever, no matter how much I appreciate you and your family's hospitality." Thinking about Angel and work caused a couple of recent events to pop into Alexis's mind.

"Right." He didn't think she'd be sticking around, did he?

"I'd like to keep in touch this time, Ryan, and I

hope we can talk about that later, but I just thought of something that might be important to the case." She tried to catch his gaze but he turned to make coffee, effectively blocking her from getting a good look at his expression.

RYAN KEPT his back to Alexis, not wanting her to see the disappointment. It came out of the blue and he chalked it up to nostalgia. The reality was that Alexis had a life in Houston. Ryan had a life on the ranch that he loved and their friendship had ended a long time ago.

It was good to see her again. Maybe he would get the closure now that had escaped him before.

"Yeah, staying in touch would be nice."

"Okay, good. Because I just remembered that Angel had been getting a few little gifts at work and, thinking back, she was really cryptic about them."

"What do you mean? What kind of gifts?" he asked.

"Things like little cards left on her chair after lunch. There was a chocolate rose left on her keyboard that I saw after my break. I thought maybe she had a secret admirer or maybe a stalker. And now I'm wondering if she wasn't having some kind of secret affair," she said.

"With someone at work?"

"Or maybe with a client. I'm not really sure. But it

seems kind of strange that she said a client recommended this place to her and she'd been really cryptic about gifts she'd been getting from someone. She would immediately hide them. I would sometimes get back from the break room before her. I kept thinking with all the extra hours we'd been working I couldn't see how she'd have time to date. Heaven knows I didn't." Her cheeks flushed and he couldn't help but think the rosy hue made her even more beautiful if that was even possible.

"If she was having a fling with someone from work, wouldn't you recognize them?" he asked.

"Yeah." She blew out a breath. "That's a good point. I mean, I don't know who all of our clients are and especially not the ones she talks to. You know how it is in Texas. It seems like the average male height is six feet. All you have to do is walk into any grocery store on a given day and you'll see someone who is big with a muscular build. Even my boss, Jeffrey, bulked up even more in the past year since his wife became sick. He said he had to work out all his frustrations at the gym while she was in treatment and he felt pretty helpless."

"Understandable." Ryan rocked his head. He couldn't imagine the woman he loved getting sick and having to undergo lengthy treatments. The only thing worse than that would be having his child go through something horrible and not feel like he would be able to help. That would be hell for any parent and he wouldn't wish it on his worst enemy.

Ryan made two cups of coffee and poured a glass of water for Alexis. He'd noticed that's what she'd taken earlier.

He double-fisted the coffee mugs and brought them along with the water over to the table where Alexis sat. "Was it possible Angel was having an affair with a married man?"

"I feel like anything's possible at this point."

"The killer was angry. It's the reason my mind kept snapping back to Darcy's ex," he admitted.

"Mine did, too. Probably because we know the killer was male. It's the easiest place to go."

"If I've learned anything from watching my brother and Ensley's case, it's that it usually winds up being the most logical person." He'd also learned there were secrets in what used to be considered a sleepy little ranching community. And those in power would do almost anything, including cover for a murderer, to protect their loved ones.

Ryan walked over to the fridge and opened the door. "There are plenty of leftovers in here."

"I'd be happy with a snack. Something light like yogurt or cereal if you have it. Nothing that's too much trouble. In fact, I can get it myself." She started to get up but he waved her off.

"I don't mind." She seemed so worried about being a pest that it was hard to do anything for her. "Letting someone help you out doesn't make you weak, by the way."

"That's not what I meant by it." She bristled and he felt another wall come up.

"Alexis, it's okay to let your guard down a little bit around me. I don't bite. It's *me*. Remember? We used to grab snacks for each other all the time. It's no big deal." The words came out a little more heated than he'd intended. It didn't take long to realize he wasn't helping matters based on the stiff reaction he got. Not the response he was going for. He was letting his frustration get the best of him. If he wanted some of those iron walls to come down, he was going to have to take another approach.

Finding the words was proving harder than he thought, so he walked over to her and sat down beside her. He looked into eyes that had changed. Those once bright baby blues had a harder edge now.

But that wasn't her. The hard edge was only covering her vulnerability. What had come so easy to them before was tough. Walls had to be broken down to get to that same place—a place there'd been peaks of in the past few hours.

He reached a hand toward her face and saw it as a good sign that she didn't flinch. She only met his stare head on, almost in a dare.

Taking the look as a sign to keep going, he brushed his finger along her jawline and toward the tuft of hair outside of her ponytail. He tucked if behind her ear and she leaned forward until their lips were within inches.

The air in the room charged with so much electricity the energy was palpable.

"I know it's been a while, Alexis. But I'm the same person as I was before." He could hear the huskiness in his own voice.

"I doubt that, Ryan. Life changes people."

Looking into her eyes was going to be his biggest downfall yet. Because he saw a glimpse of that rare vulnerability as they darkened with need.

"It's okay to lean on someone else. It doesn't make you weak."

"I'm so out of practice, Ryan. It's just been me for such a long time." More of that vulnerability came through. "Once I lost my mom I just shut down."

"You didn't have to shut everyone out." He searched her eyes and saw the hard edge starting to return.

"That's where you're wrong, Ryan. Everything I knew was going to be taken from me. My mom, my home, my friends. Graduation wasn't that far off and I barely made it through the school year. I had to toughen up to take the next step or I would've broken. Leaving here was one of the hardest things I've ever done." She stopped like she needed to catch her breath.

"People move. It doesn't mean they cut contact with everyone."

"Well, I had to. I don't have your family's money.

Life was harder for mom and me. We got by but it wasn't like I had anything left when she was gone," she said defensively.

"I won't pretend to know what you went through losing your mom; I was too young to know any different when my mom passed away. But you had me. I would've been there for you."

Alexis blew out a sharp breath and fire danced in her eyes. He expected her to argue but instead she closed the distance between them and pressed her lips against his.

10

I f Ryan had one regret it was that he hadn't asked Alexis on a date in high school. He'd picked up on signs a few times when they were both single. Whether or not he should act on them had kept him awake more nights than he wanted to think about.

Inevitably, one of them would show up a few days later with a date. At the time, he'd been too scared to ruin their friendship. A lot of good that had done. She'd walked away without looking back anyway.

Kissing her now was probably going to cost him. But with her sweet lips pressed to his, all he could think about was how right the world felt in this moment. All thoughts of whether or not this was a bad idea dissipated.

With Alexis's lips pressed to his, the battle that had been going on inside his head longer than he cared to admit waved the white flag. He surrendered.

He deepened the kiss. She tasted like vanilla mixed with his favorite dark roast coffee. He brought his hands up to her face and tilted her face toward him for better access. His pulse skyrocketed and he felt hers do the same.

The heat in that one kiss robbed his breath. It should've scared the hell out of him, especially because he wanted to keep her in his life. This might just cause her to turn tail and run.

His body had never reacted so fast. What was happening between them hinted at the promise of so much more. If anything, it stoked a fire that was already gaining ground. Despite his body screaming for more, he pulled back.

Forehead against hers, he needed a minute to catch his breath.

"That was a mistake, Ryan. I'm sorry."

"Don't do that," he quickly countered. "That was right up there with one of best kisses of my life. I won't have it spoiled by an apology." He tried to lighten the tension between them with his comment but it didn't seem to work.

"That's the problem. It was for me, too." She said the words so low he barely heard them. She could have shouted them for their impact.

"Can you trust me?"

"It's just not that simple for me."

They couldn't have a friendship without trust. His had been broken once already after she took off. He'd wondered what would happen if he ever saw her again so many times over the years. He just hadn't expected to feel this kind of draw towards her.

Ryan didn't want to feel this way toward anyone and especially not someone he couldn't trust.

Being with Alexis had been so easy in the past. They'd hung out together most of their free time because they genuinely liked each other's company. They'd shared the same twisted sense of humor. They'd laughed at the same jokes. Despite their differences, they couldn't wait to hear about the other person's day. Hell, when he really thought about it, they'd been the closest thing to a couple without actually dating.

A couple of his girlfriends over the years had had issues with the amount of time he spent with Alexis. At the time, he thought they were being possessive and a couple of them were wired that way he'd found out after a few weeks of dating.

No one had ever made the cut for long. And when any of them made him choose between them and her, he'd always picked her. Friendship had always been more important than a passing girlfriend.

"You know I can't stay here for much longer," she said.

"I'd like to go with you." He didn't want her being alone after everything she'd been through.

"I can't ask you to do that, Ryan. You have work

here and there's so much going on with your father."
She was a little quick with the protests.

"Let me ask you this. Do you really want to go
home by yourself?" He couldn't imagine that she did.

"No. I don't like taking off a Band-Aid, either, but
tugging at it slowly hurts so much worse. Sometimes
you just have to rip it off so you can deal with the
pain."

"You don't have to." With her ankle injury, she
needed someone around to take care of her and a voice
inside him said she hadn't had that since her mother
died. It also dawned on him that she was pushing him
away again.

At least this time she was giving him a chance to
counter.

"I appreciate what you're trying to do for me,
Ry—."

"Then let me." He cut her off. He wouldn't try to
force help on her. That wouldn't work and would
most likely cause her to run faster than a deer that
picked up the scent of a hunter. But he would let her
know that he wanted to help. "Your car needs
repairs."

"I thought I needed new tires." She leaned back
and picked up her coffee cup. She rolled the mug
around in her palms a few times before taking a sip. A
nervous tick?

"The battery cables were destroyed. I don't trust
that he didn't do more than that so I'd like to have it

fully examined by a mechanic before I put you back on the road."

"I have work." Her panic levels looked like they were about to shoot through the roof and that stirred his need to reassure her, to make her feel safe.

"We'll get you in something around here as a loaner until yours is safe again," he promised.

Alexis leaned back in her chair and he could almost see the wheels turning. At least she seemed to be considering it. And since any good negotiator knew when to push harder and when to walk away, he stood up and moved to the granite island in the center of the room.

"Penny has been stressed lately and you know what that means." He changed the subject before she could get too inside her head and overthink it. Ideas always worked themselves out in the back of her mind. Dwelling on a new thought only made her more resistant. He'd learned that the hard way like when she'd spun out over which colleges to apply to. She wouldn't stop overanalyzing UT versus A&M, or doing two years at community college to save money even though she might have been able to get a partial scholarship. Ryan finally convinced her to hop on back of his palomino, Cracker Jack, and let him take her for a ride. He'd surprised her by sending one of his brothers ahead to set up a picnic at his favorite spot on the lake.

Ryan set up a campfire and they roasted marshmallows for S'mores. On the ride back, with her arms wrapped around his chest, she'd proudly announced that she'd decided on community college first.

The change in subject definitely caught her off guard but she rolled with it. "Cooking and..." Her eyes lit up. "Baking."

He brought a fresh container of cookies over to the table and set it down in between them. There were several dozen.

"Oh, her chocolate chip cookies are my favorite. And the oatmeal raisin. I haven't had these in so long." Her eyes lit up and his chest puffed out a little.

"Those are still my favorite, though." He took one of the sugar cookies with vanilla frosting and sprinkles.

"She only makes those at Christmas. Awww, she must be really struggling."

"Penny has been very worried about Dad. We all are. We just deal with it differently."

Alexis picked up a chocolate chip cookie.

"Getting back to Angel. You never saw her chatting with a particular person? Or being quiet on the phone?" he asked.

"Not really. She kept a pretty tight lid on whatever it was. I figured she was seeing somebody and keeping it on the downlow. You know, like maybe she didn't want everyone to know she was in a relationship."

"People can surprise you." That was all Ryan said as he picked up his coffee cup and took a sip.

Rogue had followed him into the kitchen. Ryan got up and walked over to the treat jar. He got one of those pea-sized training treats for his buddy. Rogue had come a long way since being that scared little rescue who'd rarely left his cage and had almost no human contact. He'd grown into a confident dog. Ryan chalked up some of the success to the fact that Rogue was still young when he'd been rescued. If he'd been much older the changes in him wouldn't have been so drastic. Ryan wouldn't have cared or turned an older dog away. He was going to get a better life no matter what. This gave Rogue a chance at a fuller life.

Footsteps sounded in the hallway and A.J. appeared with Tuck right behind him.

"Does the name Dave Reynolds ring any bells?" A.J. asked Alexis.

"Yes. I know for a fact he's a client. He and Jeffrey have known each other for a lot of years. I didn't work with him, but I definitely know that name. He stayed with Jeffrey even through his wife's illness. I never took over that account."

"Would Angel have spoken to him?"

"Absolutely. She handled the finances for every campaign, not just my clients. I stepped in for Jeffrey in a lot of cases but there were certain clients that had been around for a while that Jeffrey kept."

"Dave Reynolds fits the physical description. He came a month ago and rented the cabin by himself. He would've known the layout. He stayed four night and five days. He was a late check-in so he asked for the key to be left under the mat. I got his ID. Do you want to take a look and see if he seems familiar to you?"

Alexis was already on her feet. She hobbled and almost took a spill but grabbed onto the back of the chair to right herself.

Ryan moved beside her and offered his arm. He still felt burned from their conversation a few minutes ago. And his mood wasn't helped by the fact that electricity sizzled where her hands touched his skin. It was best to ignore it for the time being, because he refused to live the hell of losing her twice.

"I'll just turn the screen around." A.J. got to the laptop first. He turned the screen around and held it out so Alexis could get a better view.

Ryan felt the shudder that rocked her body.

"It was so dark. I couldn't swear it was him. But that is Dave Reynolds in the picture. I saw him come up to meet with Jeffrey a time or two. And he is large. Again, Ryan and I were just talking about how tall and substantial was a pretty average description in Texas"

Ryan had a few questions for this Dave Reynolds character. Questions he figured it would be difficult to ask without interfering with an ongoing murder investigation. One thing was certain, if this guy was connected to Alexis's job then Ryan needed to talk her out of going back to work. At least until the killer was caught.

Or he could work on the angle of her letting him go

home with her. He had no problem driving her to work for a few days. Houston was only a few hours away.

All he ever did at the hospital was pace the hallways. Being there for his dad was important, but him and his brothers were bad at sitting around and waiting. Penny was covering a lot of that for them, spending most of her time at the hospital. Only coming home to shower, rest and cook.

But then home ran like a well-oiled machine because of her. She had the ranch running like clockwork.

ALEXIS STARED AT THE SCREEN. Another jolt of frustration and fear rocked her. Dave Reynolds. She didn't *know* him, but she'd probably passed him in the hallway more than once on his way to meet with Jeffrey. It was creepy that the killer could be someone from work. She'd been so fixated on Darcy's ex that she hadn't seriously considered anyone else.

She also noted that Stevie Patterson didn't fit the width of the person she'd bumped into in the hallway.

The murderer had literally suffocated the air out of Angel and Darcy by stuffing pillows over their faces. He must have moved so quickly. She had to think maybe they would've fought back. Maybe there would be evidence underneath their nails.

"I keep running through the crime in my mind and

all I can think is that they had to have fought back. I mean, Angel was the kind of person to stand up for herself. Darcy, I couldn't tell you. But her sister wasn't the roll over and let someone hurt her or sister without fighting back."

"It's possible we'll find DNA evidence underneath their fingernails or that we'll be able to find some sort of hair sample to match but part of DNA technology is unreliable. It's not like on TV. Investigations can take months. The perp would have to have a record that could be matched up to and if Dave Reynolds is our guy, he's a businessman. He might not have any priors. In fact, he would have a lot to lose if word got out about a relationship with someone at an office where he did business. There could be a wife in the background. Kids," Tuck stated. "If this was his first kill, it's highly unlikely he'd be in the system. Stevie Patterson is a little bit easier to line up if we find any hair fibers from him on the scene. That kind of evidence is more damning because he had no reason to be on the property."

Tuck's explanations made perfect sense and she didn't think an investigation would be as smooth and easy as they were on TV. It was a little bit alarming that DNA evidence could take weeks or possibly months to get a match back. She knew they would track down Stevie Patterson, and now they had another name to work with, Dave Reynolds.

"Do you know if Dave brought anything with him? Like a dirt bike?" she asked.

"No. He was a pretty standard fishing client. Rented the cabin for a few days and I didn't see him much," A.J. said.

"I did," Ryan admitted. "I recognize him."

Alexis didn't like the edge in his voice. It made the hairs on the back of her neck stand on end.

"I saw him moving around the property, fishing pole in hand. I didn't think much of it at the time. He might have been scoping the place out and even planting a few things to use later. He might have been planning something like this for a while." Ryan reached down and scratched Rogue behind the ears.

"Did you interact with him?" A.J. asked.

"No. But you already know how I feel about this whole rental situation."

A.J. bristled. He put a hand in the air. "I think it's safe to say this place is off the market. In fact, I'd be a fan of tearing down the building once the deputy and sheriff get what they need."

"We'd have to mention to the others but I'm on board with that. The cabin is old, outdated, and I can't imagine renting it out to anybody after what happened. And that's if anyone in their right mind would even want to rent it out."

"You might be surprised," Tuck said. "Folks can be pretty macabre."

"Let's just say that I don't want that kind of element on the ranch," Ryan added.

Alexis had seen it firsthand when Ensley's younger brother had died in the woods. There had been ghost stories of him haunting that part of the area and every Halloween, he was mentioned along with his friend who also died. There was always some jerk teenager from a neighboring town who thought it would be a good idea to go into the woods with a cell phone and a flashlight. Tuck was right. People could be pretty macabre and especially teenagers whose brains hadn't fully developed anyway.

"When will you be able to talk to this Dave Reynolds?" Ryan asked.

"I need to update Sheriff Justice. Patterson isn't exactly off the hook, but his priority is dropping on the suspect list since he doesn't fit the general description of the person we're looking for." Tuck picked up his notebook and made a few more notes on it. His cell buzzed and he checked the screen.

He looked up at Alexis.

"The sheriff said you can have your personal belongings back. She's sending someone to the big house with them. You might want to check your cell messages. She said your phone has been buzzing every few minutes."

11

"Thank you for bringing these to the house, Hawk." Ryan shook the ranch foreman's hand. Hawk wasn't having it and brought Ryan into a bear hug instead. Hawk, Ryan's brothers and cousins, along with his father and Penny were part of the many reasons Ryan had never felt a need to leave home.

Being in Cattle Cove had its disadvantages. Dating was one of them. There'd been plenty of women who'd made it known they'd like to go out with Ryan but finding that special one had always alluded him.

Trust was important. He couldn't see himself spending the rest of his life with someone he couldn't trust. Plenty of women in Cattle Cove knew his family and wanted to date a McGannon, and for some of them, they didn't care which one.

Since he didn't get off the ranch much and to a

town where his last name didn't follow him, he'd been limited on relationships. It was easy to see through the ones who went out with him for the wrong reasons.

He'd met a few in Austin he wouldn't mind spending more time with. The problem always showed up when he started comparing his date to Alexis. It was damn near impossible for anyone to measure up. He wanted to be with someone who rocked his world on every level. He wanted to be with someone he could talk to about anything. He wanted to be with someone who made him look forward to coming home to every day.

Too many folks settled in relationships. He'd seen it with a few of his buddies. Worse yet, he'd watched on the sidelines when some of his own family members married for the right reasons only to end in divorce.

The bar for him had been set at someone he could see as his best friend and equal partner. He needed to be with someone who was intelligent and beautiful, both inside and out.

So, yeah, his standard was pretty high. He also believed that marriage was for life. It didn't always work out that way but he would never go into a relationship thinking he'd take it for a test drive and get divorced if it didn't turn out the way he'd hoped.

"Any word from Penny?" Hawk asked, breaking him out of his revelry. There was something brewing behind Hawk's eyes when he mentioned Penny that caught Ryan's attention. Logically, Hawk was asking about Dad, but he also seemed concerned about Penny and how the situation was affecting her.

Good. Penny had looked after everyone for so long and they all did their best to return the favor but Ryan, his brothers, and their cousins were like her kids. Hawk was closer in age. She spent so much time on the ranch, this was her life and her family. She'd never had a lot of friends and it struck Ryan that he was just now noticing.

"Nothing yet, which means there's no change." He knew she would put a message on the group chat that she'd created, one that Hawk was on, in case anyone had news about their father during their shift at the hospital.

"Is she doing all right?" Hawk asked.

"As well as can be expected. You know her. We all think we're tough but she's probably the strongest one among us."

"That's the gospel truth." Hawk nodded and smiled. He nodded toward Alexis who had taken her belongings and sat down in the living room. She was thumbing through messages on her cell "How about Alexis?"

"She's a tougher nut to crack," he said so low she wouldn't hear him.

"On the outside, she's tough as nails but I see that same young woman who had a heart so big she seemed to feel everyone else's pain." Hawk's observation was potent. "Be patient with her. Sometimes the ones who need us the most push us away the hardest."

Ryan took those words to heart. "I don't want to smother her but I don't like the idea of her going to Houston alone. I also don't want to leave while Dad's in the hospital."

"Maybe this will help," Hawk began. "You love your father and he knows it better than anyone. He has all of us in his corner and company round-the-clock." Hawk paused and his gaze narrowed. "Who does she have?"

"Me."

"That's right. She has you. Let that sink in for a minute." Hawk's words slammed into Ryan with the force of a tornado, shredding him. She'd been alone for a long time now. She wasn't used to depending on anyone else.

There was no way he would try to force her to accept his help. But she needed to know that it was available, and she needed convincing that it was okay to accept a hand-up.

When Ryan really thought about it, he could stay plugged into the family. As much as he wanted to be there when his dad woke up, he could get updates. Alexis had her cousin and his family, but were they really in her corner? Would they fight for her or leave her to her own devices?

He suspected she'd be on her own. She'd been on her own and had gotten very good at dealing with life that way. And, yes, she'd pushed him away but at least he understood her reasoning. The thought of getting close to her only to be shut out again scared the hell out of him, too.

He'd already compared every other woman he'd dated to the Alexis he'd grown up with. That person was gone. She'd changed, but not so much the girl he'd known wasn't still in there.

Plus, she'd just been through unimaginable trauma. He couldn't force her to stay at the ranch. He couldn't force her to let him go home with her. But he could reason with her and hope to push past her walls. He could let her know how much he wanted to be there for her and would always be.

He wouldn't sleep at night without knowing she was going to be all right, and that the bastard who'd killed Angel and Darcy was behind bars. And if someone connected to her office was responsible, he needed to talk to her about the possibility of taking some time off from work. He needed to see if that was feasible.

Ryan wasn't sure how well that conversation would go but Alexis was smart, and despite being shaken she was sensible.

"I better get to the bunkhouse and check on the boys." Hawk referred to all the of ranch hands as his boys. Being in his late fifties gave him a few rights most people didn't get. That was one of them. Hawk considered everyone who worked for him one of his boys.

Most of the ranch hands were in their late teens or early twenties, so they were more like young men. Being called one of Hawk's boys was a compliment. "Let me know if you need anything else today. Otherwise, I'll keep everyone working before I swing by the hospital and pick up Penny."

"Will do, Hawk." The man deserved to be called *uncle* more than Donny. Ryan also took note of the fact Hawk was Penny's ride home.

As Hawk walked out the front door, Uncle Donny walked inside.

"Hey, Ry," Uncle Donny said and the air in the room became tense.

"Sir." Being called *Ry* was fingernails on a chalkboard to Ryan. Alexis shot a look that Uncle Donny couldn't see but Ryan understood. One eyebrow up and her head cocked to the side, lips pursed she made eyes at him. Basically, the expression meant *what an idiot*.

Ryan couldn't agree more. He nodded as Uncle Donny obliviously walked past before making a show of saluting in the direction of the living room. The man stopped in his tracks when he saw Tuck and A.J. huddled over a laptop.

"Good evening, gentlemen," he said to them both with a nod toward Alexis.

A.J. stood because that's the way he was brought up. Same for Alexis. Tuck stood so he could walk over and shake Donny's hand in an obligatory move.

"Everything all right?" Donny asked, looking from Tuck to A.J.

"Trouble at the rental cabin today," A.J. informed. He spoke to Uncle Donny out of respect for their father's wishes but Ryan knew his brother well enough to see he'd forced a smile.

"Nothing too big, I hope." Donny was filthy from working outside and Penny would have a fit if she saw him walk through the front door covered in dirt.

"Actually, it is." A.J. gave him the quick run of events.

Uncle Donny's shock was written all over his face. He'd never been a suspect due to his size and, honestly, Ryan didn't want to think his flesh and blood could do something so evil. "I'm real sorry this happened. If there's anything I can do to help with the investigation..."

"The sheriff's office will be in contact if there is," Tuck said.

"Sheriff Justice already asked me to stop by her office in the morning. Do you know if this is the reason?" Uncle Donny asked Tuck.

"No, sir." Tuck looked like he drew a blank. Even if he knew, it wasn't likely that he could tell Donny. But his sincerity said he didn't.

"All right then." Uncle Donny loved those three words. "Good seeing everyone. Now, if you'll excuse me. I need to get cleaned up. I'm planning an early dinner before my shift at the hospital."

His comment was met with nods and forced smiles. He excused himself and moved down the hallway. Uncle Donny was never left alone in the hospital with Dad. No one said it outright but if he couldn't be trusted in the equipment room then no one wanted him alone in the hospital.

Ryan decided to stay right where he was in the hallway, so Donny couldn't try to listen to their conversation. He wasn't sure why he didn't want his uncle in on the murder case. The man was too old and short to be responsible for the murders. But Uncle Donny was the kind of person who left people a little unsettled after he left a room.

ALEXIS STARED AT HER PHONE, flipping through messages from Jeffrey. Her boss was understandably concerned about her. Twenty-seven messages seemed like overkill. She wasn't in the mood to talk, so she sent back a text saying she was okay, that she was with friends, and would call him as soon as she felt able to talk. Her cell immediately buzzed, indicating a call was coming in—her boss.

She appreciated his worry, but she really wasn't in the mood to talk about what had happened and he needed to respect her space. But then, she'd always dropped everything at a moment's notice when he needed her. Come to think of it, she'd done that with her cousin, too.

She rejected the call. If anything, his persistence was showing her that she wasn't ready to face the world. There were other messages and phone calls, too.

She put her phone to her ear and listened to the first voicemail.

What she'd been through was making the wheels turn in the back of her mind. She'd also been thinking a lot about what Ryan said. Did she really want to go home alone? The short answer? No. But she'd gotten so good at depending on no one but herself that she was really bad at letting others help her.

If he still wanted to go home with her until she got her bearings again, she wanted to let him. She realized more than ever that she needed a friend. The tricky part was keeping him in the friend zone. Because the way her heart stirred every time he was in the room made her realize those feelings she'd felt years ago were very much alive and well.

She hadn't known what to do with them back then and she sure didn't know what to do with them now. For now, she'd try to pick up on their friendship. She'd missed that the most. Just being able to pick up the phone and talk to someone who knew her, who *really* knew her would be a welcomed change from the way she'd been living.

Despite having a room in her cousin's house, she'd

never felt close to him or his wife. Maybe it was because they were newly married, but she felt like the odd man out. Burying herself in school, work and then helping them had left her exhausted at the end of the day. Connecting with anyone socially back then hadn't exactly been a priority. She'd just been trying to get through the days.

Being back on the ranch, she realized how much this place felt like home and how much she'd missed that feeling.

Refocusing on her phone, she saw that message after message by reporters wanting to ask questions about the double murder. She had no idea how they got her personal cell phone number except that having anything remain private these days seemed next to impossible. She also wondered if Jeffrey had given it out, without realizing the upset it would cause in her life. It was impossible not to feel like this was an invasion of privacy.

"Ryan," was all she had to say and the next thing she knew he was right by her side. She handed over her cell.

His face said it all as he listened to the messages and then read text after text. His lips thinned. His brows furrowed. White hot anger flashed in his eyes. He issued a sharp breath when he moved the phone away from his ear and then looked at her.

There was a storm brewing behind his eyes and it

looked like he was having a rough time trying to hold it back.

"If your offer to come home with me still stands, I'd like to take you up on it," she said.

"After hearing these, I had no plans of letting you out of my sight."

Those words shouldn't comfort her as much as they did. She was used to depending on herself. But being around someone she could trust to have her back kept her nerves below panic levels.

"We should probably go soon." She wanted to get home and climb under the blanket. Sleep might be tricky because the events kept replaying in her mind. Her ankle roared with pain.

With Ryan at her place, she would feel comfortable enough to take another painkiller. Those made her tired anyway and might be just what she needed to push her over the edge.

"I'll grab an overnight bag." He looked toward Tuck and A.J. "Are we okay if I take off?"

"We'll let you know if anything else comes up in the investigation or we have any additional questions," Tuck said.

"We're all good here," A.J. added.

Ryan thanked them before offering a hand-up to Alexis. She took it and then leaned some of her weight on him. Her ankle wasn't happy about all the sitting she'd been doing without elevating it. She needed to remember to ice it later.

Ryan led her to his room. "I've been keeping clothes here since my dad's accident, in case I need to sleep over or head straight to the hospital after working the ranch. My house is a half-hour drive from the big house."

"Makes sense."

"Hold on just a few minutes while I grab an overnight bag and throw a few supplies inside." His room was just as she'd remembered. Massive king-size bed along one wall. A study desk and chair near the window. A dresser. All the wood pieces had been carved by hand and had his room looking like something out of a magazine spread.

It was kept in perfect order. He pulled a bag from the closet and dropped it onto the bed. He retrieved a handgun and holster from a lockbox and placed them inside the leather bag. The fact he might need to use a weapon reminded her of the danger lurking.

The killer got what he came for...right? What reason would he have to come back for her? She tried to shake off the creepy-crawly feeling climbing up her back and couldn't. His words haunted her.

You weren't supposed to be here.

12

Alexis leaned her head against the headrest of Ryan's truck and napped on and off during the ride to Houston. Every once in a while, she'd wake with a start and have to get her bearings again. All Ryan could do was offer quiet reassurances. She was okay. He wasn't going to let anything happen to her.

Shock seemed like it was beginning to wear off and he needed to watch that. As strong as she was, she'd experience unimaginable trauma. He didn't care how strong she was, she was going to be affected. Being strong only made her want to hold it all inside. He knew a thing or two about that.

Rogue slept in between them, and Ryan noticed that Alexis kept her hand against his dog's leg. The fact Rogue seemed to bring her comfort shouldn't make him feel as good as it did. He wanted her and Rogue to be close.

Her place was a two-bedroom bungalow just north of Houston. He pulled onto the quiet suburban street as she sat up straighter.

"Are we already here?" she asked, rubbing her eyes and yawning.

"Looks like it. According to the GPS we're on your street." The fact she'd been able to sleep at all was good. Although, her brain was mostly likely going into reserve energy mode because she wasn't getting enough deep sleep. At least she trusted him enough to doze off.

He pulled in front of her house. The front yard was fenced and that most likely meant the back was as well. Homeowners liked six-foot privacy fences in this area. Although, they had suburbs where he lived, most people had chain link fences. Not being able to look out and see for a block without interference was strange. It was late and it was dark outside but there were plenty of streetlights to light the area.

As far as picking a safe environment, she'd done well. The block suited her with its neat row of bungalow-style houses and well-manicured lawns. Ryan was much more for open spaces and skies that went on forever, but this suited a lot of people and it wasn't his place to judge.

"I'm that one." She pointed to the house his GPS was taking them to anyway.

It was to the right in a cul-de-sac. He pulled up in front.

"I can manage on my own. You have a lot to carry in," she said.

"Or I can make two trips. The extra walking is nice after being in the car for a few hours," he admitted. It felt good to stretch his legs. Rogue hopped out behind him and he realized he'd forgotten to put on the dog's leash. Considering it was so late, he thought he might be okay.

Until movement caught Rogue's eye and he dashed toward it. A few seconds later, Ryan realized his dog had chased a squirrel up a tree. At least Rogue wasn't barking and waking up the neighbors. Neighbors were another reason Ryan could never see himself living in the city. He glanced around. They were way too close for his liking.

Ryan leashed Rogue and then followed Alexis into her home. She stopped a couple of steps into the foyer and flipped on the light.

"Something is off." She looked around the space and then shrugged.

Taking a couple of steps, she turned to face him. There was a blank look on her face.

"This is weird. I can't place it but something is different." She looked at the couple pair of neatly lined up shoes against the wall next to the door.

Holding onto the wall, she bent forward. Her gaze zeroed in on a particular pair of tennis shoes.

"Does something look different to you about these?" she asked.

"Other than the fact they're paired backwards?"

"That's exactly it. I would never place my shoes like that."

Looking around the apartment, noticing everything had a place, he agreed with her assessment. "Is it possible you were in a hurry and flipped the shoes by accident?"

"It's technically possible for me to walk on the moon someday but it's highly unlikely."

"Okay. Then, stay here with Rogue." Ryan set his overnight bag down next to him and took a knee. He opened the bag and pulled out his weapon. He looked at Rogue. "Stay."

Ears up, Rogue looked very concerned. Dogs seemed able to pick up on the slightest shift in energy.

Ryan kept his body near the wall and moved through the space, clearing each room. He checked window latches and the lock to the back door. Nothing seemed out of the ordinary. By the time he reached the living room, Alexis had moved to the chair to sit. Her ankle was propped up on a pillow and her tense face muscles gave him the impression she was in a lot of pain.

Rogue kept her company and he'd never been prouder of the animal that had become his best friend.

"The place is clear, and I didn't see any signs of a break-in. Does an ex-boyfriend have a key, by chance?"

Those words sent fire stalking through his veins despite the fact she was single and her dating life both past and present was her business. She had a past. He had a past. That was life.

"No. I would never do that."

As much as those words sent relief shooting through him, they also made him realize that she hadn't just shut herself off to Cattle Cove. She'd locked out the world.

Was he any different? By keeping his standards so high no one could reach them, he'd pushed everyone away, too.

He guessed they had a lot more in common than he realized.

"What about your landlord?" he asked. "Does he or she have a key?"

"I own the place." She flashed eyes at him. "Well, I have a mortgage, so technically the bank and I are equal partners, but they don't own a key."

"There are devices nowadays that can get past almost any lock without breaking it."

She shot him another look.

"A skilled burglar can bypass almost any security system."

"Makes you wonder how anyone can be safe even in their own homes." She glanced down at Rogue. "You probably wouldn't be willing to part with this guy."

"Nope." There was no hesitation on that answer. "I

am willing to let you come by the ranch anytime and see him."

"Thanks. I'll probably take you up on that. I feel like I've made a new friend through all this craziness."

"Looks like he feels the same."

"I may have found a new partner in crime." She smiled but her expression quickly morphed. She blew out a sharp breath. "When did everything get so complicated, Ryan?"

Ryan wished he could answer that question. For her. For his own family.

"I'm looking forward to sleeping in my own bed but after the nap on the way over and the excitement once we got here, I'm wired," she admitted.

Ryan was on edge. He couldn't ignore the fact someone had entered the cabin without breaking in. There'd been no sign of forced entry.

He glanced around the tidy space. There was a leather sofa—the kind he could really sink into—and one of those recliners that looked more like a chair.

A bookcase took up the entire opposite wall and had barn doors that were partially opened to a large flat screen television. There were just enough feminine touches in the room to suit her personality. She was casual, easy-going and beautiful beyond words. Her home reflected every bit of who she was inside and out.

"And this ankle is screaming. I seriously doubt it will let me sleep."

"Ice will help. I can grab it if—"

Alexis opened her mouth to stop him and then seemed to think better of it when she compressed her lips and cocked her head to one side. "You know what? I'd appreciate any help you're willing to give. I can keep my ankle propped up with a pillow. Ice is in the kitchen."

He smiled. This was progress. He'd take it.

Ryan moved into the kitchen and opened a couple of cabinets, the pantry and the fridge to get his bearings.

It didn't take long for him to locate supplies. Ice was the obvious one but he also found a plastic freezer bag and a clean dish towel. He loaded up the plastic bag with ice and brought it into the living room.

Alexis had moved to the sofa. As promised, her foot was propped up on the chunky wooden coffee table resting on a pillow.

"Think you can eat anything?" He went to work positioning the ice bag on her ankle and then wrapped it with the clean dish towel to secure the pack.

"I can try." She winced as she readjusted her foot.

The ankle was swollen and he probably needed to take her to get it checked out in the morning.

"I saw a few things in there I can make, or there's a pizza in the freezer. Or fixings for an omelet if you're not in the mood for pizza."

"Are you kidding me right now? You'd make me one of your famous omelets?"

He chuckled. "I saw cheese, eggs and milk. There was spinach in the produce drawer. As long as it's fresh, I'm good to go."

"It should be. I was only going to be gone for the weekend and I didn't want to shop before I had to go back to work. So, I ordered some food and stopped by the store to pick it up."

He shot her a look.

"Oh, right. You don't have grocery deliver on the ranch. Of course, you don't need it because you have pretty much everything you could ever want out there."

"Not everything," he countered, not adding that *she* wasn't there anymore. But he was just torturing himself with that wish. Looking around her place, she'd made a home in Houston.

"You have food for days."

"You won't get an argument out of me there," he said, trying to cover for his slip.

"Convenience isn't a bad thing, Ryan. Like you said, there's pizza in the freezer but we could also call for delivery."

"Why would we do that?" he shot back.

She rolled her eyes at him but clamped her mouth shut.

"I wouldn't want to make you miss out on my omelet."

"Not a chance," she countered.

He chuckled. The lighter conversation broke some

of the tension and stress of the day. It was nice to see her smile again and look like she meant it.

He'd fed Rogue before they left the big house, so he was good to go.

"I'll see what I can whip up for you." He turned to leave the room.

"Ryan?"

He stopped.

"What do you think about watching a movie?"

"Only if there's popcorn," he joked. He couldn't remember the last time he sat on the couch and watched a movie. He didn't watch a lot of sports. He'd always enjoyed playing baseball more than viewing it. He caught a few games during football season. He kept the game on in the background while he worked around his house.

Ryan moved to the kitchen, gathered supplies and whipped up one of his famous omelets. He located bread and then made toast with a little jelly on it just like he remembered Alexis used to like.

A cutting board would do as a makeshift food tray. He put the plate and silverware on it along with a paper towel to use as a napkin.

She looked up at him with those blue eyes that had a really bad habit of making his heart freefall.

"This really takes me back. Thank you for this." There was a glimpse of the real Alexis in there. Despite always being the shy girl in class, she had one of the biggest personalities once he got past the external layers. He wouldn't say that was an easy job. It took time to get to know Alexis beyond a surface level.

He was just pointing out that it was worth it.

Ryan went to get his own plate. He stood in her kitchen and finished his off, needing a minute because damned if his heart didn't betray logic every time he got a glimpse of the smile behind the wall. He checked her pantry where she used to always keep medicine. He grabbed the ibuprofen bottle before filling a water glass.

"I thought these might be better than the painkiller that knocks you out and makes you nauseous." He remembered the time Alexis got a hairline fracture in her wrist during PE when Juliana Rock came down on top of her during volleyball. Her mom was working an overnight shift, so they'd convinced her to allow Alexis to stay at the main house so Penny could look after her.

The pain medicine made her so sick she got no rest. Ryan had stayed up with her, making an excuse about needing to study for a Chem test. He knew Alexis was sick when she didn't call him out on it. And he'd sat by her side as she dry heaved. Hair piled on top of her head, she'd been sheet white for most of the night.

She'd told him that she couldn't decide what was worse, being in pain or being nauseous all the time.

"I remember. I'm just surprised you do." She practically beamed up at him.

"We had a lot of good memories, Alexis. And I

hadn't really thought about most of them in a really long time. It's kind of nice to think back."

"We have a lot of history," she said and there was a distant quality to her voice that he didn't like.

"We do."

"I've missed it," she said under her breath. She said the words so low that he barely heard them.

Yeah. Me, too.

Being with her again reminded him of all the times they'd had together. All the late-night texts and early-morning rides to school. It reminded him how easy it should be to be around someone. The dates he'd had in recent years always seemed like so much work. Having a conversation felt like a job except that he had more fun working the ranch than he did on dates.

The last few years, he'd put less effort into dating. Every date had been starting to feel like the same. Same restaurant. Same conversation starters. Same bone-deep wish to be somewhere else.

He kept pushing through because, like everyone, he wanted to find someone he could lock in with. No one measured up to his standards.

And that was probably Alexis's fault.

13

Alexis felt a whole lot better after eating and taking ibuprofen. Ryan had made popcorn and brought it in a bowl along with a couple bottles of water that he set in between them.

The easy way they were talking and joking reminded her so much of old times. It also made her aware of what she'd been missing out on all these years.

She held up the remote. "What do you want to watch?"

"I don't care as long as it's not boring."

"You always did like action movies." She playfully threw an elbow into his ribs and he was dramatic about it, clutching his side.

"When did you stop liking them?" he asked.

She bit her bottom lip. "Normally, I'd be all-in.

Tonight, I think I need something a little more relaxing."

"How about something funny?"

"I can go for a comedian." She flipped through the channels until she found one her favorites. "Have you seen this one before?"

"I don't really get a chance to watch a whole lot of TV. You'd be safe showing me pretty much anything." He picked up a kernel of popcorn and tossed it into his mouth.

"You can still do that?"

"Looks like it," he said on a chuckle. He sat so close their outer thighs touched and warmth spread through her body. "I haven't done a lot of things I used to since you left town."

Alexis left that comment alone. Her cell kept buzzing through the intro of the comedy act. It was most likely more texts from her boss.

"Do you want me to get that for you?" He nodded toward her purse.

"I'm pretty certain it's my boss. I said I didn't want to talk. I'll see him on Monday."

"Have you considered not going back to work for a while?" he asked.

"I'd hate to leave him in a bad position since his wife—"

"Didn't you say he had help with her now?"

"Yes. But—"

"And you told him that you were fine already." He

didn't may eye contact but frustration came off him in waves.

She started to argue but then bit her bottom lip instead. The fact Jeffrey was concerned about her was probably a good thing. Right? One of her coworkers and his employees had been killed along with her sister.

Angel didn't talk much about her personal life outside of work but then Alexis figured there wasn't much to discuss.

"Have you thought about taking a few days off?" Ryan asked.

"Not really."

"I don't have to be the one to tell you that you just went through hell. The effects of that might last longer than you realize." Those words struck a chord.

A knock sounded at the front door. Alexis gasped and Rogue went full-on attention. She started to move but Ryan put his hand on her shoulder, so she stopped.

"Do you want me to answer that?" he asked.

She nodded. Putting any weight on that ankle would only cause it to scream at her even more, her pulse had skyrocketed and her heart was in her throat.

He moved to the door with athletic grace and Rogue on his heels. He opened it and she could see from where she sat that it was Jeffrey. A glance at the clock revealed that it was after midnight.

Jeffrey seemed startled by Ryan and Rogue. She could only imagine how intimidating the two of them would be to an outsider. And it was probably because of what she'd been through in the past twenty-four hours, but she liked seeing her boss hesitate before making a case for showing up this late.

"Can I help you?" Ryan's curt tone made Jeffrey tense up even more. Despite going to the gym and buffing up over the past six months or so, Jeffrey was no match for Ryan's size. Jeffrey barely came in at five-feet-ten-inches if she had to guess. Whereas Ryan was a solid six-feet-four.

He glanced around nervously and then his gaze landed on Alexis. Eyes wide, he shot her a look of panic. She expected him to be surprised but his reaction seemed over the top.

"I stopped by to check on Alexis." His voice practically shook. Nerves? Concern? Something else?

Ryan folded his arms over his chest and glanced over at her.

"It's okay. He can come inside." She nodded.

Jeffrey didn't seem so certain that he wanted to after sizing up Ryan and Rogue. Ryan took half a step back and then reached back to hold onto Rogue's collar to stop him from charging forward. His hackles were raised and a low growl tore from his throat. There was just barely enough space for Jeffrey to squeeze through.

Her boss would be considered good looking by most standards. He was on the tall side. He had sandy-blond hair and dark blue eyes. He was tan with a runner's build.

"How are you?" He couldn't get away from Ryan and Rogue fast enough.

She shot him a desperate look. How should she be after what had happened?

"I meant physically. Are you hurt?" He stared at her ankle.

"It's not as bad as it looks. It'll be better in a few days." Instinct told her not to tell him just how damaged her ankle might be. But why did she have the urge to protect herself from her boss? Wasn't he at her house out of concern for her? Why did his multiple text messages and phone calls rub her the wrong way?

Because she feared he was covering tracks for a friend?

"Okay. Take your time coming back to work. I know I've leaned heavily on you in the past year but—"

"Taken advantage of is more like it," Ryan said low and under his breath.

Jeffrey must've heard but he railroaded the comment. "I apologize for..." He seemed to be searching for the right words. "*Everything* that's happened."

"Did you know Angel had a secret admirer at work?" she asked Jeffrey, not wanting to give up too much information but also testing the waters to see what he knew.

"No," he said quickly. Too quickly? "How do you know?"

"She talked about him the other night."

"Did she say who he was? I'll fire him on the spot." Jeffrey shifted his weight from foot to foot and crossed his arms over his chest. He repeatedly looked over his shoulder toward the closed front door and beads of sweat formed on his forehead.

"I'm afraid not."

Her boss's gaze kept darting around. This was more than concern. But what? Jeffrey couldn't have been the one in the cabin. He wasn't big enough and she would've recognized his voice immediately even if it was low.

"Do you think she was having an affair with a client?" he asked.

"She didn't mention names. I know someone was leaving cards and flowers on her desk, so someone had access to the building."

His hands were balled into fists and he kept cracking his knuckles. His eyes were wild. Did he know about Angel and Dave Reynolds? She had no plans to mention the name. The two had a long history and went way back. She couldn't help but wonder if her boss had shown up to see if Dave was a suspect. Maybe he thought he could get inside information about the investigation from her.

"Is there anything else you need to ask, or can I show you out the door?" Ryan walked into the living room and stood next to Alexis. Rogue immediately made a move toward Jeffrey, who jumped and immediately took a couple of steps backward.

"I'm good. Like I said, I only came to check on Alexis and let her know she can take all the time she needs before coming back to work." Jeffrey couldn't find the door handle fast enough.

"I appreciate you coming by," Alexis said. She saw a completely different side to her boss than before. She'd noticed changes in him but had dismissed them as what he'd been going through with his wife's illness. Now, she had questions.

"I've been concerned about you, Alexis." Those words shouldn't sound sinister. And yet they did.

Was he concerned about her? Or concerned about covering for his friend?

RYAN LOCKED the door behind Alexis's boss and then immediately turned to her. He studied her for a few seconds before reclaiming his seat next to her on the couch.

"Rogue didn't like your boss." His dog wasn't the only one.

"I got that distinct impression." She grabbed a throw pillow and hugged it against her chest. "He was off."

"I've never met the man before, but he sure seemed

nervous." Ryan didn't like how shocked Jeffrey was that he and Rogue were there. Had he been expecting to find her alone? Had he been counting on it? If he was involved, he had to know her tires had been sliced.

"Yeah, it would be impossible not to notice that with the way he kept cracking his knuckles and shifting his weight."

"He seems guilty of something." Ryan couldn't figure out if he was an accomplice or trying to cover for his friends. "Dave Reynolds is at the top of my suspect list."

"We should call the sheriff and let her know what just happened," she said.

"I was just about to suggest the same thing. You're certain the guy from the cabin wasn't your boss, right?"

"Yes. That guy was a lot taller and more substantial than Jeffrey. I would have known him right away despite the changes he's made in the past few months," she admitted.

"What kind of changes?"

"Since his wife got sick, he started working out. He said it was to ease some of his pent-up frustration about her illness."

There were other reasons a married man suddenly started a workout routine. None of which had to do with his wife. "Do you know if they had a solid marriage?"

"I never really asked. Not long after I took the job, she got sick."

"So, the changes in him...are they recent?" He didn't like where this was headed.

"Probably over the past six months or so. They've been dealing with her sickness for almost a year now." Her head was tilted to one side, which meant her wheels were spinning. "You don't think..."

Her voice trailed off like she couldn't voice something so unfathomable as a man cheating on his sick wife.

"We'll have to let the sheriff decide. In the meantime, I think you should take a few days off work. The place will keep running without you—"

"I need this job, Ryan. I have a mortgage and other bills. I have a little safety net but it's not much." He could see panic rising in her eyes. "I know there are bigger issues to deal with here and, believe me, I know the stakes. But I'm also the only one keeping a roof over my head. I spent most of my savings on the down payment on this place and I can't afford not to get a paycheck."

"Hey, you're not alone anymore. Remember?" He took her hand in his to offer reassurance and felt a surge that rocketed up his arm, through his body and pulsed hard in the center of his chest.

She looked at their hands and then blinked at him. In that moment, he knew she'd felt it, too. But then chemistry didn't seem to be a problem between the two of them. Trust. Oddly enough, was harder to come by.

"I would never ask you for money."

"You wouldn't have to. But that's not what I had in mind. My family has a good name with a lot of connections around Texas. I was thinking a job referral from a McGannon wouldn't hurt. Plus, we could help put the word out that you're looking. I know you, Alexis, any company would be lucky to have you." He could tell by the smile that tugged at the corners of her mouth he was getting through.

She cocked her head to the side and compressed her lips. The wheels were spinning, and he wasn't sure what to expect.

"I'd appreciate that, Ryan."

"Deal." He wouldn't look a gift horse in the mouth. "As for now, let's update the sheriff and then get you to bed."

She shot him a look at the last part.

Now, it was Ryan's turn to smile.

"You know I didn't mean it like that," he added real fast. And he could have sworn he heard her mutter, *that's a shame.*

She phoned Sheriff Justice and relayed what had just happened. And then Ryan helped her up and to her bedroom.

"I need a few minutes to clean up. Do you mind staying in here?" she asked.

"As soon as I let Rogue outside to do his business." Ryan waited for the okay from Alexis before retracing his steps down the hallway and double checking that he'd locked the front door.

"Let's go, boy." He turned on the porch light and stepped into the cool night air. Spring on a cattle ranch was the busiest time of year and with everything going on with Dad everyone pitched in to make the business run smoothly.

Even Uncle Donny seemed to be on his best behavior lately. Of course, if he'd paid attention to what was happening in the equipment building, they might have avoided Pops' injuries being so drastic.

Ryan didn't even want to consider the possibility that his uncle might have done something to Pops or 'helped' the accident along. He was the one who'd called 9-1-1 and Ryan had to believe the man cared.

Despite his older brother, Levi, not trusting Uncle Donny as far as he could throw him, Ryan didn't want to believe the man was capable of something that sinister. Time would tell. As soon as Pops woke up, he could tell his side of the story. Of course, he'd taken a serious blow to the head, and the doctors had warned that he might not be able to remember much.

There were other possibilities that might come with traumatic brain injury that Ryan couldn't fathom. Like his father having to learn to walk and talk all over again. He might not remember who he was, let alone recall his kids.

No one could be certain what Pops would be able to do until he came out of the coma. Thinking about it caused frustration to burn his gut. He wanted to be able to do something for Pops. There wasn't much worse than being stuck in a hospital as far as he was concerned. And it was hell to watch a man who'd been so strong and full of life just lie in bed all day and night. It was gut-wrenching to see Pops still and like he wasn't even there, with only a machine to force keeping him breathing.

Ryan had never been much on prayers, but he said one for Pops tonight while standing under the stars. There was too much light pollution to see them clearly but that didn't mean they weren't there.

His dog took a couple laps around the backyard before bolting toward him after Ryan whistled. He scanned the backyard. The tall privacy fence would keep neighbors out, but animals would find a way in if they wanted to.

A crash sounded in the house. Now, it was Ryan's turn to bolt inside.

14

"What happened?" Ryan had taken the extra second to lock the back door but he stood in the doorway to the bathroom, looking at Alexis who was trying to pull herself up on the counter.

"My ankle. It gave out. I tried to put too much weight on it. I'm not usually so clumsy." She'd been a runner in high school. Not for the school team. She ran for herself and no one else.

He'd always like that about her. It was part of the reason he'd quit baseball. There'd been too many expectations that had drained the fun out of the sport. Yeah, he was athletic. And, yeah, he could throw a ball. His favorite games were the ones played in his own backyard on the diamond Pops had built. He thought back to the games they'd played with his brothers and cousins on Sunday afternoons. The grill was always going and the smell of fresh burgers filled the air.

"Let me help you up." He offered a hand, forcing his gaze away from the towel that was slipping off her silky skin.

Embarrassment heated her cheeks as she held it together and it made her even more beautiful. His heart took another hit. Much more this evening and he wouldn't survive until tomorrow.

She grabbed onto his arm and he helped her to her feet. The towel stayed put but he'd touched enough of her silky skin to know how much trouble he was in. Then again, his attraction to Alexis was already a slippery slope.

Her skin was wet so she must've tried to take a quick shower. He stood there while she brushed her teeth and he turned his back toward her when she got dressed.

"Thanks for coming home with me, Ryan."

"Hold on a minute," he teased. "Are you about to say that I was right?"

"Afraid so."

"Well, it's good that you're not denying my brilliance, finally."

"No one said you were brilliant. I just said you were right," she quickly countered, wiggling an eyebrow and clucking her tongue. "Those aren't necessarily the same things. Even an idiot would be right at least part of the time statistically speaking."

He wrapped his arms around her waist and picked her up fireman style. Hearing her laugh made his night as he carried her into the next room and set her down on the bed.

"How's that for being a caveman?" he teased.

She fluffed a pillow behind her. "It wasn't bad. I've been carried by stronger men, but you didn't drop me, so...good job."

He feigned insult.

Rogue hopped up on the foot of the bed and made himself comfortable, curling in a ball at Alexis's feet.

"I think he likes me better than you," she quipped.

"Oh yeah? That might be true but he's still my dog."

She snapped her fingers. "He seems really comfortable here."

"He'd be lost without me." Ryan turned to his dog. "Right, Rogue?"

The animal picked that moment to snore.

"I guess he has spoken. He stays." She folded her arms and pouted. He wanted to bend over and claim those sweet lips again. He'd gotten skilled at resisting temptation when it came to Alexis. They were getting their footing as friends and he wouldn't do anything to ruin it.

Of course, when she grabbed his shirt and tugged him toward her, he didn't fight her despite the warning sirens going off in the back of his mind. And when his lips met hers one word came to mind, *home*.

Ryan captured her mouth with his and she gave a little moan of pleasure that stirred him in more than one place.

Rather than get too wrapped up in the moment, he pulled back and feathered a kiss on her chin, her jawline and down her neck before pushing off the bed and walking into the bathroom.

A shower later, he'd washed up, brushed up and was ready for bed.

"I can take the couch. It was comfortable enough for me to get a good night's sleep," he said.

"Would you mind staying in here?"

"I can do that." Ryan crossed his arms and pulled the hem of his T-shirt, tugging it over his head. He tossed it onto a chair next to the bed and climbed in beside her.

She curled up against him and he wrapped his arm around her. His senses were flooded with her clean flowery scent and that wasn't going to make it easy to sleep.

Her steady, even breathing came a few minutes later.

The sun was up before Ryan opened his eyes again. He hadn't slept through a sunrise in longer than he could remember.

Glancing at the clock, he realized it was almost ten

o'clock. He'd slept the day away. Having Alexis in his arms, he couldn't complain. She'd thrown her leg over him at some point while they'd slept. Her warm, silky skin against his was waking up other parts of him best left alone.

It took a second for him to peel her off and slide out of the covers without disturbing her. She needed sleep. Apparently, so did Rogue because he was out until Ryan started moving. Then, the dog perked up. He hopped off the bed and stretched.

Ryan walked as quiet as he could toward the kitchen. He needed caffeine and food. He went right to work on the first.

While he waited on the coffee machine to work its magic, he made toast. Once he had a fresh cup in his hand and a couple of sips down, he could think more clearly.

Of course, that's the moment Alexis walked into the room. She smiled at him and it seemed like the most natural thing to wake up together.

"Morning," she said as she walked past him. She was able to put weight a little weight on her injured ankle. Ice and rest really were miracle cures.

"More like afternoon," he teased. "Coffee's fresh if you want some."

"I could smell it. It's what woke me up. Best way to wake up, by the way." She grabbed a mug and filled it. She made that same little mewl sound when she had her first taste of coffee that was so damn sexy. It reminded him of the taste of those pink lips of hers.

And since that train of thought was about as productive as trying to get pennies from an ATM machine, he boxed them up and set them aside.

"Somehow I'm sure you've had plenty of coffee brought to you in bed." He was only half teasing and he didn't like hearing the sound of those words.

"Not a chance. No one sleeps over and I don't stay overnight at anyone else's house." She seemed to catch herself mid-admission. "Last night was definitely an exception. It's not like you're..."

"A date." He finished the sentence for her as his cell buzzed. He moved over to where he'd left it on the kitchen table and picked it up. "It's an update from Tuck."

She bent down on her right knee and reached for Rogue, who was by her side. "And?"

"He says Dave Reynolds has a motorcycle license and that he doesn't want you anywhere near him until they can clear him or lock him up."

"Oh." Eyes wide, she one-fisted her coffee mug as she absently stroked Rogue's fur with her left hand. Taking his dog home shouldn't feel like betraying her. When the time came to split up, it wasn't going to be easy to separate those two without breaking Ryan's heart. They were becoming inseparable and he hated to be the one to break up the party.

Ryan returned the text, thanking Tuck for the heads-up.

THE PICTURE EMERGING SENT an icy chill down Alexis's back. Angel was having an affair with Dave Reynolds, he'd murdered her and her sister, and her boss was trying to cover for his friend.

Consequences be damned.

"Jeffrey must've stopped by last night to see if I knew anything. I passed by Dave Reynolds in the hallway. They must be wondering if I put two-and-two together," she said.

"Or finish the job for Dave."

"He said that I wasn't supposed to be there. And I wasn't. He must have known Angel and her sister were staying there for the weekend. He had to have been the one who'd referred her to the place."

"She could've been there with him before when he stayed at the cabin. It's possible that I didn't see her. I mainly check on the place in the mornings," he said.

"You being here really shocked Jeffrey." The look on his face last night gave him away.

"And shook him up. He couldn't get out of here fast enough once he got a good look at me and Rogue."

"It does make me question whether or not he's more involved than we realize. I hope he was only stopping by for information." They'd never know now.

And she was grateful because being around him at all had been creepy.

She couldn't imagine ever going back to that office again. Not with this information coming to light. And yet the part of her that had always refused to cave to bullies wanted to march right into her boss's office and demand answers.

"I wonder if Tuck checked out Jeffrey's personal affairs," she said.

"How did business seem?" he asked.

"Financially?" she asked.

He immediately nodded in response.

"They seemed okay to me but then I'm not sure I would know any different. My paychecks came through wire transfer and there haven't been any problems that I know of," she said.

"With you home and one of his employees..." he cast his eyes at her, "*gone*, he'd most likely be at work right now."

"True." She cocked her head to one side, trying to figure out where this was going.

"How well do you know his wife?"

"Lisanne? Not very well." But she had a feeling she was about to get to know the woman a little better.

"Do you know where she lives?" His question said she was right on track.

"Yes. I had to run papers by their house one day a couple of months ago. I have the address in my phone. I don't know about disturbing her, though. She's still really sick and her sister is there. She might not let us see Lisanne."

"It never hurts to stop by and check."

She didn't bring up the point that it might just get her fired. She could make up some excuse about needing to stop by and talk to Jeffrey. She could pretend that she didn't realize he might be at work.

"Give me fifteen minutes and I'll be ready to go." She walked gingerly on her left foot toward her bathroom, still feeling the burn from her injury.

As promised, it only took a few minutes to dress in joggers, a sports bra and camisole T-shirt. She threw on a little lipstick to brighten her face and try to bring some sense of normalcy to her routine. She brushed her hair and let it fall over her shoulders.

The only reason she was willing to disturb a very ill woman was to get answers for Angel and Darcy. Since Jeffrey was such a close friend with Dave Reynolds, Lisanne had to have met him. At the very least, she could give them a little more information about him.

As much as Alexis believed in honesty, she would be willing to fudge her reasons for dropping by unexpectedly based on the dire circumstances.

She could say that she needed to find out more about Dave for a file she was working on. Okay, that sounded like a flimsy excuse to stop by. If it was that transparent to Alexis, she wouldn't fool anyone else. She'd have to think of a better reason for the visit on the way over.

In the kitchen, Ryan stood with Rogue by the sink. He drained his cup of coffee and she did her level best to shift her focus away from his strong back. By the time she made it to the kitchen, Ryan handed over a to-go sandwich and cup of coffee for her.

"I thought you could use a bite on the road," he said.

Rather than thank him with words, she walked over and kissed him on the cheek. With him around, she was beginning to believe that she might not be as alone as she'd felt for more than a decade.

She was beginning to see that cutting herself off from everyone and everything she'd loved only hurt her more in the long run. She'd paid a hefty price but, in her grief, didn't see any other way.

"What was that for?" Ryan said, his eyes darkening with something that looked a lot like need.

"Reminding me what it is for someone to have my back for a change." And she would have his, too. That was a two-way street as far as she was concerned. "You've already done so much for me and I know that I can't begin to repay my debt to you."

"You don't owe me anything," he said all casual and everything that was Ryan McGannon. "It's what friends do."

She made a funny face at him. "You might not say that if you ever tasted my cooking. I should probably be barred from the kitchen."

He laughed, a low rumble in his chest.

"It's good to know some things never change," he quipped in the smart-aleck tone that could only belong to him.

"How do you know it's not a ploy to get you to cook all the meals?" she teased.

"I've tasted your cooking, Alexis. I wouldn't feed it to Uncle Donny." He kept a straight face as he walked right past her toward the front door.

"That was a low blow. Even for you, McGannon." She laughed, appreciating the break in tension.

Because nothing inside her wanted to bother Lisanne while she was recovering.

15

A lexis kept one hand on Rogue and the other on the door handle. She kept a steady tap rhythm with her fingers, looking keenly aware of the fact they were about to intrude on a sick person's life.

The lighter banter had died down after they got inside the pickup and stress came off Alexis in palpable waves. He didn't like the idea of going to her boss's house anymore than she seemed to, but he couldn't think of a faster or better way to get information about Dave Reynolds.

The sheriff was doing her job but, in his experience, investigations took time. Weeks could pass without progress. Since the murders had occurred on McGannon property *and* involved someone he cared about, he had no plans to sit back on his heels and wait. Not to mention the fact that Dave Reynold's fingerprints would most likely already be on the property. Since he'd stayed there, a good defense attorney could have a field day if that was used as primary evidence.

Besides, Alexis wouldn't sleep at night until the bastard was locked behind bars. And if that *person* happened to be tied to her boss, hell would have no fury to match Ryan's.

Knowing that, he would step aside and allow law enforcement to do their jobs. His only hope was to help them get there faster by doing a little investigating on his own. There'd been something niggling at the back of his mind and he couldn't for the life of him figure out what it was.

Then again, it might just be this whole case. The only bright spot—if there could be one in this much tragedy—was that the circumstances had brought Alexis back into his life. Their friendship was finding its footing. It was probably wrong to want more and especially this early. And yet, his heart didn't get the message.

It had thought holding her last night was the best night he'd had in his adult life. It had thought waking up to her was being home. It had thought there could be a chance for something more, something lifelong.

So, how was that for not cooperating with the whole friendship thing?

As far as being an idiot, Ryan was going all in and he needed to have a conversation with Alexis after this case was behind them. Because as much as he didn't want to lose her again—and he couldn't stand the thought—having her in his life on a part-time friend basis was losing its appeal.

The GPS interrupted his thoughts, indicating he should turn into the upscale neighborhood where her boss lived in The Woodlands. The street contained mini mansion after mini mansion, all different enough to be unique but uniform enough to indicate they belonged on the same street.

This was the kind of place that would have its own security, possibly its own police force, and Ryan was keenly aware of the fact because driving three miles over the speed limit could get him pulled over.

It was late morning and, given the fact that Lisanne was ill, that seemed like a good time to catch her awake.

"What does Lisanne look like?" He wanted to know in case the sister answered the door.

"I haven't seen her since she got sick, so I imagine she's changed. She might not even have hair. My description might not get us too far but here goes. The last time she came to the office, which was shortly after I first started, she was lean and athletic. I could tell she worked out on a regular basis. She has, or at least *had*, coffee-colored hair and light brown eyes."

"Like Mila Kunis?"

"Yes, and just as pretty. They look related at the

very least," she said. "Lisanne's face is a little more heart-shaped and—"

"Do you mean her?" He pointed toward the woman who'd rounded the corner and was heading in the same direction as they were.

Alexis craned her neck and swore. "Stop the truck."

He pulled over to the side of the road and parked. Alexis hopped out of the truck so fast he didn't have time to grab Rogue, who went right behind her.

Grabbing the handle and then throwing his shoulder into the driver's side door, he joined them a few moment later. Unfortunately, not before Rogue set to barking.

The look on Lisanne's face was pure shock. It mirrored the one on Alexis's.

"Lisanne?" Alexis's voice held all the shock.

Her boss's wife stopped jogging, took a couple of steps backward to inch away from Rogue, and pulled her earbuds out.

"Alexis. What are you doing here?" Lisanne asked, seemingly just as surprised by their visit.

Ryan made it to Rogue and managed to wrangle his leash on. He quieted the dog with a hand on his back and then took a knee beside him.

"What are you doing out of bed?" Alexis asked.

In her pink jogger and sports bra, Lisanne looked tan and fit. She held up her smart watch and tapped the screen. Those things could measure just about everything with the right app.

"I go for a run every day. Why?"

"You've been really sick—"

Lisanne stopped everything right there. "Hold on a minute. Who said I was still sick? I *was* sick but I got into a trial and I'm in remission. I have been for months."

She was a little on the thin side, but she looked like she was taking care of herself. Nothing about her looked terminally ill.

"Your sister." Alexis's forehead creased and she brought the pad of her hand up to touch it. "I thought she came to help out and that's why Jeffrey has been able to come back to work."

"Hold on. My sister is here but she certainly didn't come to take care of me. She's visiting while her house is redecorated." Lisanne looked like she came from family money. She seemed the kind of person who grew up with plenty and had been taught to downplay it. Like if someone asked her if her family was wealthy, she might say they did all right. That kind of coaching came with a lifetime fortune.

The real question on Ryan's mind had to do with Jeffrey. Why would he lie about his wife's health? Was he looking for sympathy? Was he enjoying the attention he must've gotten when everyone heard his wife was terminal?

Was he enjoying time off while abusing the trust of his employees?

"Is that what Jeffrey said?" There was a strong note

of contempt in Lisanne's voice. She took in a couple of deep breaths and then brought her watch up. She hit the screen a couple of times and Ryan figured she'd just ended her workout. She eyed him up and down, like she was trying to place him and couldn't. "Do you want to come inside?"

"I sure as hell do." Some of Alexis's shock seemed to be wearing off and she was finding her anger.

"I'm right here." Lisanne pointed to one of the mini mansions. She glanced at Rogue. "He stays outside."

"Then we all do," Alexis countered, and he couldn't be prouder of her than he was right then. The fact that she'd defended Rogue without hesitation sent all kinds of warmth shooting through Ryan.

"Follow me to the backyard then." Lisanne seemed more like the poodle in her purse type of dog owner.

Ryan didn't have anything against poodles. He feared he'd step on one by accident on his way to the bathroom in the middle of the night.

The four of them navigated the Mediterranean-style complex complete with manicured lawn. The place had the ambiance of a five-star hotel on a smaller scale.

Lisanne didn't seem to have any trouble walking and looked like she hadn't been sick for a very long time. This was confirmation that Jeffrey was a liar and manipulator. He'd tricked his employees into believing his wife was still undergoing treatment. Her hair was shorter than Alexis had described but long enough to realize any chemo treatments she might have had would have been long over.

Why would a man lie to his employees? It was easier than asking them to devote all their free time to his business but ultimately what did he have to gain? And what about Dave Reynolds?

When it came to murder, there was always a motive. This was a double murder. Ryan suspected Darcy was killed to cover up the real target, Angel.

Angel and Dave were connected by her job. Again, all roads led back to Jeffrey.

"WE WERE PLANNING to get a divorce before I got sick." Lisanne pointed to a sofa and chairs nestled around a coffee table under a pergola in her expansive backyard. The pool water was the clearest blue Alexis had ever seen. The whole area had a Mediterranean bar vibe.

The three of them followed Lisanne and took a seat. Alexis's mind was spinning. The woman was supposed to be on her deathbed. Showing up and finding Lisanne not only on her feet but out for a run had Alexis's thoughts churning.

Her boss was a liar. Why? What was he covering up? Surely, he wouldn't go to all this trouble to make his employees believe his wife was still sick just to milk extra hours out of them. Would he?

"Oh really?" Alexis asked, studying Lisanne. Was

there any way she could be involved? Did she know what her husband was covering up?

The woman had graced just about every society page with Jeffrey before her sickness. On close appraisal, she looked a lot thinner than Alexis remembered and the spark to her eyes was gone. Of course, she'd just confessed that she and her husband were going to split up before her illness.

"The sickness...is that why he stuck around?" she asked.

Lisanne just laughed. "That would insinuate my husband had a heart."

"Are you saying he doesn't?" Alexis hadn't really gotten to know him as a boss or a person considering he'd spent so little time at the office, but only a real jerk would use his wife's condition to squeeze extra hours from his staff.

Lisanne cocked her head to one side. "Are you saying that you haven't noticed any changes in him?"

Alexis couldn't say she knew him well enough. "Do you want to give me an example?"

"Didn't he seem awfully tan to you for the past year?" she asked.

"He said that you liked sitting by the pool and he stayed out here with you but kept forgetting to put on suntan." She hadn't asked him directly, but someone had and that was the answer that had circulated around the office.

Lisanne's half-laugh, half-chortled mocked Alexis. She bristled.

"Don't take this the wrong way. You seem like a nice person but a little naïve. My husband is tan because he goes out on the boat every weekend and he golfs during the week. He would tell you that he married into a life of luxury, but my family cut him off a couple of years ago when we caught him cheating." She crossed her arms over her chest like the memory made her defensive.

"How did you find out?"

"Private investigator." She stared into Alexis's eyes like she waited for a reaction. "Not me, of course. I was naïve enough to think my husband married me for more than my father's money."

"How long was he having the affair?"

"Months, maybe more," Lisanne said.

A thought struck that Alexis wanted to ignore. The cards at work left on Angel's desk. The flowers. The gifts. Could they have been from Jeffrey?

If only she'd pressed Angel for details that night on the back porch looking over the lake at the sunset. She might have found out that Angel had been having an affair with the boss. She might have realized sooner who the person behind the murders was...

But that couldn't be right. A cold chill raced up Alexis's spine at the thought someone could have been hired to kill Angel and her sister. She stared into

Lisanne's eyes. Were they the eyes of a coldblooded killer? A scorned woman could be ruthless.

Deadly?

If her husband was cheating and she knew it, had she decided turnabout was fair play? Of course, this theory only held true if Jeffrey was having an affair with Angel. Would she have an affair with a married man who had a sick wife?

Lisanne leaned forward like she was about to divulge a secret. "Back to your question. Did my husband stick around because he felt bad that I was sick?" The smile that crept across her lips made Alexis shudder. "The answer is no, despite what he said. He was here because as long as we were married, he stood to keep his inheritance. Daddy had Jeffrey sign a prenup. If we ever divorced, he didn't get a penny."

"What about the company?" she asked.

"Started with my family's money and, therefore, covered under the prenup." She stared at Alexis like she was sizing her up. "You know the place was in the red, right?"

Rogue must've heard something because he jumped into action. He spun around as she and Ryan followed the dog's gaze. Hackles raised, he started rapid-fire barking.

"Jeffrey?" Alexis stood along with the others. Instinct had her backing away from her boss.

"What's going on here? Did someone call a meeting

and forget to invite me?" He smiled at then and extended his arms, palms facing toward them.

"How'd you know we were here?" Alexis asked.

"Cameras," Lisanne said low. "I didn't turn them on today. He must have."

Ryan positioned his body in between Jeffrey and Alexis, she realized. Rogue was agitated but Ryan didn't look down. Instead, he bent down like he was about to calm Rogue.

In one swift motion, Jeffrey's right hand flew behind his back. Metal glinted as he brought his hand around at the same time Ryan came up with a gun from his ankle holster.

"Don't move," Ryan warned. "Put the gun down."

16

They stood there, facing off, weapons pointed at the center of each other's chests. One twitch of a finger and someone would be dead. The fact that Rogue was firing off barks seemed to escalate the tension. Alexis started toward him to calm him.

"Go back, Alexis," Ryan warned. He had her best interests at heart, and she wouldn't normally walk toward a gun pointed anywhere near her direction but there was no way she was letting anything happen to Rogue. She'd gone all-in with the animal and there was no going back now.

"It's okay. I'm taking Rogue." She kept her voice as calm as she could as she made her way toward him, hands up. "I'm just going to get his leash." She took it from Ryan gently. "And then go back where I was standing."

She took a step backward and crashed into Lisanne who was practically hiding behind Alexis. The fact her body was trembling outlined just how dangerous this situation was. She didn't trust her husband not to shoot.

"If you go through with this, you'll end up with nothing," Ryan warned. He seemed to have clued into the fact Jeffrey seemed to be all about money. At least from his wife's perspective. "You'll be broke, just like before. And then what?"

"Shut up." Jeffrey's voice was almost hysterical now. The fact that he seemed to be panicking wasn't good. Alexis might not know a lot about guns, but she realized it wasn't like on television or in the movies. Even if Ryan fired the first shot and scored a hit, which at this distance wouldn't be too difficult, Jeffrey wouldn't go down immediately. It would take time for the news he'd been hit to travel to his brain. He could shoot and kill all of them before he dropped.

A dark cloud pressed down on Alexis's shoulders as she worked to keep Rogue from going for Jeffrey. Her boss wouldn't think twice about shooting the animal and there was no way in hell Alexis or Ryan would allow that to happen.

"He's lost it. He's crazy," Lisanne said low and in Alexis's ear.

"Do you have any weapons out here?" Alexis asked quietly as she took another couple of steps.

"That's far enough," Jeffrey warned. Then, he

looked at a spot right behind her and added, "It's about time you got here."

The snick of a bullet engaging in the chamber of a gun sounded behind Alexis's left ear.

"What the hell are you doing?" The voice. *That voice.* She'd recognize that voice anywhere. The man from the cabin.

She started to move but he pressed the cold barrel of his piston to her left temple. Lisanne gasped.

"Shoot her and I'll take at least one of you down, probably both," Ryan warned. "And if, by chance, either of you are left standing, you'll spend the rest of your life behind bars."

Tension filled the air like a thick early morning fog in the mountains.

"I doubt any one of you will be alive to testify," Jeffrey shot back.

"Dave...you're involved in this?" Lisanne sounded shocked.

"He's the *reason* for this," Jeffrey snarled. "He couldn't stick to the plan—"

"I'm not the one who slept with her. I'm not the one who couldn't keep his pants zipped," Dave shot back. Hearing his voice again sent a cold chill down Alexis's back.

Alexis looked around for something...*anything* she could use as a weapon. The yard was fenced in by a brick wall. Plants and shrubs covered the barrier that was too high for Rogue to jump.

Even if she could break away from Dave, she couldn't outrun a bullet. At close range, it would be too easy for one of those bastards to fire and score a hit.

"Cheating with yet another woman?" Fury vibrated from Lisanne as she stalked toward her husband.

"Don't come any closer," Jeffrey warned, taking a couple of steps back. There was something present in his voice...fear?

Holding a gun and threatening someone was one thing. Shooting someone in cold blood was another. Dave had killed twice already. It was clear that he was capable of murder. Was Jeffrey?

Ryan stepped in Lisanne's path, blocking her on her way toward Jeffrey. Dave raised the barrel of his gun toward Lisanne.

"No," Alexis shouted. There was no time to debate her actions as she threw her elbow into Dave's arm to throw off his aim.

His weapon fired a wild shot as Rogue spun around and lunged toward Dave. Between her and the large animal diving at Dave, they managed to knock him off balance. He kept a tight grip on the butt of the gun and Alexis made a grab for it.

A shot fired nearby, and she had no idea if it was Ryan or Jeffrey. She heard an animal-like growl that sounded like it came from Lisanne. There was a lot of shouting but it was Dave's grunt that she heard right before he kicked her.

Dave screamed out in pain as Rogue's teeth

clamped down hard on his arm. He twisted around on the ground, trying to break the dog's grip but Rogue was relentless. Dave managed to knock Alexis's hand off him for a second.

She clawed for purchase.

In the confusion, she took a jab to the cheek and a knee to her stomach. She fought back, scratching Dave's face before he got hold of her finger and bit.

It was her turn to scream as she jerked her finger away. Rogue growled as he held his grip on Dave's arm. But then the man engaged in a death roll, breaking free from Alexis and knocking Rogue off with a yelp.

All Alexis heard next was a string of angry curses.

RYAN HAD SUBDUED Jeffrey in a matter of minutes, knocking him out the second he got close enough to slam his fist into his face. The guy was a coward and had accidentally fired a shot when Lisanne attacked like a wild banshee.

The problem had been pulling the scorned woman off her husband while she tried to bash his face in with a rock. There was no way Ryan would let her beat the man to death. Jeffrey needed to spend the rest of his life behind bars for his involvement in the murders of Angel and Darcy Pruitt. Death was too easy of an escape. Justice needed to be served.

Panic had struck when he'd heard the shot fired

from behind. Rogue's growls had intensified, and Alexis had screamed in pain.

When Ryan got over to her, Dave was in a death roll and Rogue yelped in pain. Fire shot through Ryan's veins at the sight. He released a string of curses aimed a Dave. Tucking his own weapon inside his ankle holster, he dove on top of the man.

"Can you get Rogue?" he asked Alexis.

"I'll try," came the fast response.

For now, Ryan needed to focus on Dave. The man was much larger than Jeffrey and a helluva lot stronger. He also held a pistol in his hand. So, Ryan would go for that first. Using all his strength, he grabbed Dave's wrist on his right hand.

Unfortunately, that left a whole of Dave's other parts free and available for use. And Dave took advantage of the move by launching rapid-fire kicks anywhere he could hit. The torrent battered Ryan's legs and a foot came dangerously close to the place no one wanted to be kicked.

Dave was strong and powerful. A man with everything to lose made a formidable opponent.

Ryan pulled his left hand back, made a fist, and punched Dave in the face. The man's head snapped to the side and blood squirted from his nose. Broken?

Good. Ryan had no plans to take it easy on this bastard.

Except the move was gas to a fire for Dave. He tried

to pull that death spin again, but Ryan squeezed powerful thighs to hold the guy in place.

Ryan felt something tug at his ankle and then he heard, "Freeze or I'll shoot."

Alexis stood over Ryan and Dave. Her feet were spread apart and her gaze was locked onto Dave where the barrel of Ryan's gun pointed.

Both men heaved for air. Alexis was also winded but the fire in her eyes said she'd pull the trigger if she had to.

"Drop it. And I mean *now*." There was no shakiness to her tone. This was the voice of a woman who'd been through hell and back, who'd lost friends and was done with the perp.

Dave's body relaxed. He let go of his grip on the pistol.

She took a step forward and kicked the weapon away from them.

"I should shoot you now for Angel and Darcy," she said through clenched teeth.

"He would deserve it. But don't do it, Alexis. You'd have to live with killing a man when you could've walked away," Ryan reasoned.

"There's no bringing back the people he killed. Maybe he deserves a death sentence, too." Her body trembled from adrenaline and anger, not fear. Make no mistake about it, the woman was fierce.

"He deserves to spend the rest of his life in prison."

A determined look passed behind Alexis's eyes. Sirens sounded, roaring toward them.

"I had my cell in my pocket. I called the cops," she said.

Dave's lips thinned as resolution seemed to settled in.

Yeah, he was going to jail. He was going to be locked in a cage for the rest of his natural life if Ryan had anything to say about it.

Sirens neared, the sound of squad cars doors opening and closing filled the air. Lisanne's voice broke through the noise, guiding police to the scene.

"Put your hands in the air where I can see them," a cop demanded.

As Alexis put her hands in the air, she said to Dave, "Justice is going to be served. And I hope it's Angel and Darcy's faces that you see at night every time you close your eyes while you're locked up."

The officers moved in as Alexis set the gun down, kicked it toward them, and then took a few steps back as instructed. A female officer came and patted her down as Lisanne explained that Alexis was innocent. Ryan did the same as he was relieved of sitting on Dave Reynolds.

"All of this was for money," Lisanne said quietly. "I'm guessing once we dig into the books at the agency, we'll uncover their scheme. My husband seems to have ruined his own plans by not being able to stop himself from sleeping with his employees. Some husband."

"I'm sorry," Alexis said and she truly felt sorry for the woman.

Ryan finished giving his statement and walked over with Rogue. Alexis bent down to pet him, and he wagged his tail. A crushing thought struck that he would go back to his life and she would go to hers.

17

"Do you need a ride home, ma'am," an officer asked as he approached Alexis.

"I can take you home," Ryan offered, figuring he could help her get settled before heading back to the ranch to get cleaned up and then going to the hospital to check on his dad.

"Okay," was all she said. Her cheek was the color of fire where it looked like she'd taken a hit. Her arm was scratched and she had tufts of grass in her hair from fighting Dave. Adrenaline had worn off. She'd given her statement. It was time to go home.

The officer nodded and turned toward his squad car. Ryan leashed Rogue and walked with Alexis toward his pickup. His cell buzzed. He fished it out of his pocket and checked the screen. A call from A.J. was coming in.

"Hey, what's up?" he asked his brother.

"Tuck just called. Are you guys okay, man?" The concern in his brother's voice was a physical punch. Ryan should've called or texted to let him know they were all right. He should've realized word would get back quickly through law enforcement. The minute Tuck heard a report involving Alexis or Ryan, he would've started making calls.

"We're good," he confirmed.

"Thank heaven for small miracles." A.J.'s relief was palpable. He released a slow breath. "Officers are at the agency now, digging into the files."

"That's fast for a judge to issue a warrant." Ryan opened the vehicle's door for Alexis, who climbed in after Rogue.

He moved to the driver's side.

"They didn't need one. His wife is part owner in the business. She's cooperating fully with the investigation, offering complete access to the company and to the books," A.J. informed.

"She said he was after money. Sounds like they'll find a trail." Ryan started the engine and his brother's voice filled the cab. "It could provide motive for the murder. Alexis's co-worker was heavily involved in the finances. It's believed she figured out what was going on and confronted Jeffrey."

"He admitted to having an affair with her," Ryan said.

"Tuck mentioned that." A.J. dropped his tone when he asked, "How's Alexis?"

"I'm okay," she answered, but she sounded numb. "At least, I will be."

"We're on our way to her place. I'll get her settled and head toward the ranch." The words tasted bitter, but this was the deal. He'd help her and then move on.

The thought caused his chest to squeeze and his lungs felt like they were clawing for air. This seemed like a good time to remember that they'd agreed to stay in touch.

Was it going to be enough for him?

"I'll let you go but I'll be sure to let everyone know the two of you are okay," A.J. promised.

"Thanks," Ryan said before ending the call by telling his brother he loved him. It was routine but he realized Alexis had drawn in a breath and then stared out the passenger window.

Hawk's words came back like a rogue storm. *Who does she have?*

He tried not to overthink those words as he pulled in front of her house. He parked and she was out the passenger side before he could get around to open the door for her. He offered an arm and she took it, leaning a good portion of her weight on him.

"You know what, I think I know what happened," she said before moving to the edge of her porch and bending over a plant. "Look at this."

She pointed to a dirt stain that made it obvious the plant had been moved. She picked up the pot and grabbed her spare key. "This must be how Jeffrey or

Dave, whoever it was, got into my house. I totally forgot about leaving this key here after I moved in. I won't make that mistake again."

She pocketed the key and led them inside. She turned to Ryan and said, "You can head out if you want. It's a long drive and I don't want to keep you."

Damned if those words weren't knives to the chest. Was she pushing him away again? It sure felt like it.

Ryan looked at Rogue and then Alexis. He couldn't imagine the two of them apart. They'd bonded and were practically glued to each other's side. And since he couldn't exactly disappoint his best four-legged friend, he came up with an idea.

"Alexis, these last few years have been the worst without you in my life," he started, struggling to find the right words. "It's like I've been walking around in a daze and I can't find my way out no matter how hard I try."

She stood there. Patient. Quiet. Unreadable.

"I've missed you in a way that's so much more than losing a buddy. When you left, you took a piece of my heart with you and no one has been able to fill that void. Not until now." Man, he was searching her gaze for a hint that what he was saying was okay, was welcomed.

"Rogue here doesn't want to be without you another day." He brought his gaze up to meet hers. "And neither do I."

A slow smile spread across those full pink lips of

hers and it was the first sign she wasn't going to laugh him out of her house. She fisted her right hand and placed it on her hip.

"What exactly are you saying, Ryan?" It was good to see some of that spark return to her eyes when she challenged him.

He wanted to see a whole lot more of that and for the rest of his life.

"That it's obvious Rogue here loves you, and there's no way he's giving me up. The only logical solution is to move in together right away." He wrapped his arms around her and picked her up, so they'd be eye level. She made broken look beautiful and she was stronger than she knew.

Alexis tunneled her fingers in his hair. "You love me?"

"I'm in love with you, Alexis. There's a big difference."

She stirred everything good inside him and made him want to go down that road with her, the one that lead to forever.

"You coming back into my life is a gamechanger for me. And I don't think Rogue can live without you. So, what do you think? Do you want to move in together? I don't care where we live. I'll move into your house if that'll make you happy. I just don't think Rogue could take joint custody, and I don't see any other way to make him happy than to be together."

"For Rogue's sake?" More of that smile crept across

her lips, lips he was ready to claim the minute she said *yes.*

"And mine." He feathered a kiss on the dimple in her chin. "I'd be lost without you."

"Are you sure you're not doing this just for Rogue's sake?" She looked him dead in the eye and his heart stuttered again.

"Positive." There was no hesitation. "This one is for me."

She dipped her head down and kissed him. Her lips moved against his and one word came to mind, *home.*

There would never come a time when he didn't want to hold her just like this. She locked gazes with him.

"Ryan, I never stopped loving you. I think my heart knew a long time ago that we were supposed to be together and I fought it. I was afraid of losing you if I brought up how I felt. I've been in love with you since high school. When I left, I had to shut down every-thing I was feeling to survive, and I've been numb ever since. Until now. Until you came back in my life"

"Then I have another proposal." He set her down gently, careful she could support her weight on her left ankle before he took a knee.

Holding her hands in his, he asked, "Will you do me the great honor of marrying me? I love you and want to spend the rest of our lives together. We've been apart long enough as far as I'm concerned. I want to spend forever showing you how much I love you."

Tears streaked her cheeks as she smiled and said the only word he needed to hear, "Yes."

Ryan stood up and kissed his future bride.

She pulled back first. "I have one request."

"Name it. Anything I have is yours."

"I'd like to live at the ranch," she said.

"Are you sure about that? I don't want you to feel like you're giving anything up," he said.

"Being at the ranch with you is the only time I've ever truly felt like I was home, Ryan. It's where I want to start our family and continue on the McGannon legacy for another generation." The way she beamed up at him filled his heart.

"Does that mean you'll work right alongside me?" he asked, hoping for one answer but knowing he'd be fine no matter what, as long as he got to come home to her every night.

"It sure does. I want to be equal partners in every sense of the word." Those blue eyes of hers, so clear, so beautiful were home.

"I can't imagine a better way to spend forever." He'd finally found the person he wanted to do the rest of his life with. He'd found where he belonged. And he planned to spend every day for the rest of his life showing her how much she meant to him.

18

EPILOGUE

"That neighbor is going to work my last nerve." A.J. McGannon crumpled up the note that his neighbor Tess Clemente had left for him. She was threatening to get a court order to have him cut down trees that had been planted long before she'd been born. Really?

She wouldn't dare.

Those trees weren't hurting her equipment building's foundation. A.J. glanced down at the dog sleeping at his feet. Bear, his four-year-old Newfoundland, seemed unfazed as he lay there stretched out like he owned the place, and he did. His snores echoed in the otherwise quiet office.

A knock interrupted A.J.'s tirade about Tess before it could really get going.

"Come in," he said as Bear scrambled to his feet.

He was loyal and protective, and no one got through the door without his approval.

"Saw the light on." His brother, Ryan, walked into the office. Bear jogged over, tail wagging. "Wondered which crazy brother or cousin of mine was up at this late hour."

"Or early, depending on how you look at it." A.J. chuckled as he glanced at the clock on the wall. It read two-thirty. He picked up the wadded piece of paper on top of his desk. "Got another love note from our favorite neighbor."

"Ouch." Ryan winced and then they both laughed. "What's stuck up her craw this time?"

"Same old, same old."

"Trees again?" Ryan asked.

"Seems so. She must've run out of other reasons to give me grief." A.J. chunked the wad toward the trash bucket that was a few feet away. The paper ball hit the rim and then fell inside. He pushed to standing, pumping his fists in the air. "Right on the buzzer. Another win for McGannon."

Ryan shook his head and laughed louder. "We both know that was a lucky shot."

"Doesn't matter. Points count the same," he quipped.

His brother leaned against the desk and stopped laughing. He crossed his arms as he brought his index finger to his lips. With a most serious expression, he said, "Have you considered the possibility that Tess Clemente has a crush on you?"

"Uh, no." Ryan's whole body involuntarily shivered. The comment was almost comical.

"Well, it might be time to embrace the obvious," Ryan continued, straight-faced as ever. "She's not bad looking, if you can get past that personality of hers."

"I need more than a pretty face, bro." All kidding aside, it was true. A.J. had always been attracted to intelligence and someone with a sense of humor. An attractive package was the cherry on top as far as he was concerned. Personality, sex appeal, values, those were more important than blind beauty. Don't get him wrong, he'd dated his fair share of beautiful women. He'd learned a long time ago there had to be substance for a person to be truly attractive.

Ryan cocked an eyebrow. "So, you have checked her out?"

"No. Yes." He stammered. "Hell, you're the one who brought her up. And, besides, I don't have it in me to fight with someone for an hour or bring in lawyers to decide which restaurant to choose."

His need to overexplain was digging a deeper grave.

"So, you have been thinking about her?" Ryan teased.

Well, this conversation was going downhill fast.

"What did you say you wanted?" A.J. turned the tables on his brother.

"Nothing," Ryan conceded. "Couldn't sleep."

"You're not second-guessing marrying Alexis, are you? Because I've never seen a sillier grin on your face than when you're with her."

"No. It's nothing like that. I love her. What we have is the real deal. No question there," he said with confidence A.J. didn't think he'd ever have when it came to his relationships with the opposite sex.

"What then?" he asked.

Ryan shrugged, his 'tell' that he was stalling for time. That only happened when he was about to discuss something emotional. And then A.J. realized where this was going...their dad.

"I just wish he would wake up. You know?" Ryan's question was rhetorical.

"Yeah," A.J. answered anyway. "I know exactly what you mean."

"We're holding off on the real ceremony until Dad can attend." Sadness clouded his brother's eyes. He coughed, like he was covering for clearing emotion from knotting in his throat. "It's just not the same without him."

"No, it's not," A.J. agreed. "I know he's really proud of you, though. Alexis is the best possible person for you and there's going to be a lot of reasons to celebrate once Dad gets out of the worst of this."

A.J., like his brothers, couldn't process any other outcome, knowing full well that the longer their dad stayed in a coma the worse the prognosis became. At this point, they were banking on a miracle since they'd stop counting how many weeks had passed since the accident.

"Thanks. It means a lot to hear you say that," Ryan said, walking over and pulling A.J. into a bear hug.

"We'll get through this together," A.J. reassured.

"That we will." Ryan took a step back. He tucked his hands in his front pockets as he looked over at A.J.'s trash can and nodded. "What do you plan to do about our neighbor and that note?"

"Try not to strangle her," A.J. joked.

To continue reading A.J. and Tess's story, click here.

ALSO BY BARB HAN

Kidnapped at Christmas

Murder and Mistletoe

Bulletproof Christmas

For more of Barb's books, visit www.BarbHan.com.

ABOUT THE AUTHOR

Barb Han is a USA TODAY and Publisher's Weekly Bestselling Author. Reviewers have called her books "heartfelt" and "exciting."

Barb lives in Texas--her true north--with her adventurous family, a poodle mix and a spunky rescue who is often referred to as a hot mess. She is the proud owner of too many books (if there is such a thing). When not writing, she can be found exploring Manhattan, on a mountain either hiking or skiing depending on the season, or swimming in her own backyard.

Sign up for Barb's newsletter at www.BarbHan.com.

CPSIA information can be obtained
at www.ICGtesting.com
Printed in the USA
LVHW111406090621
689797LV00012B/263